OSWAIN AND THE SECRET OF THE LOST ISLAND

For Samuel

Oswain
and the
Secret of the
Lost Island

JOHN HOUGHTON

KINGSWAY PUBLICATIONS
EASTBOURNE

First published 1990 as *Tergan's Lair*
This substantially revised edition 2002

ISBN 0 85476 970 6

Published by
KINGSWAY PUBLICATIONS
Lottbridge Drove, Eastbourne BN23 6NT, England.
Email: books@kingsway.co.uk

Book design and production for the publishers by
Bookprint Creative Services, P.O. Box 827, BN21 3YJ, England.
Printed in Great Britain.

Contents

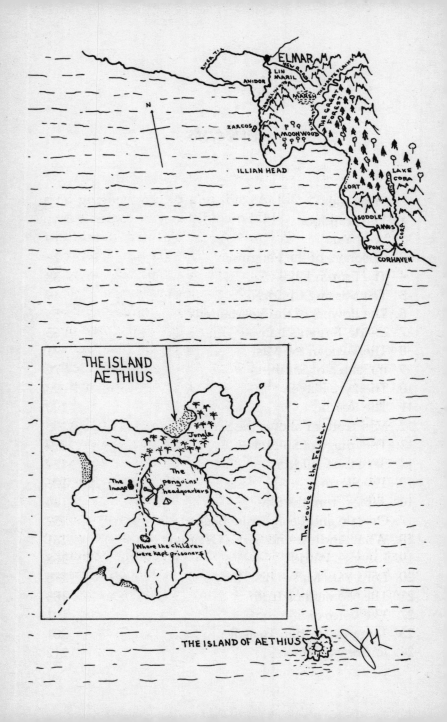

THE ISLAND
AETHIUS

Jungle

The
Image

The
penguins'
headquarters

Where the children
were kept prisoners

THE ISLAND OF AETHIUS

Prologue

Everything was still. As still as a picture hanging on a wall. And it was cold. So cold that you couldn't even shiver. A sleeping landscape, sculptured out of the deepest blue shadows was slowly waking to a new day. Sarah Brown stood watching, and her eyes were as solemn and still as the scene that lay before her.

The light when it came was sudden and brilliant: in a moment the shadows were transformed into mile upon mile of tumbled, frozen wasteland, crystalline crags and snowy cornices blinding white in the sun which seared above the horizon. Awesomely beautiful; but nothing moved.

Sarah felt that she was the only living being in the world. It was a lonely feeling. She had no idea how long she remained watching the sight. It could have been a minute, an hour, or the whole of her life. Time was frozen, just like the silent wastes that lay before her.

However long it was, it came to an end when something caught her attention. It was a slight movement at first, hardly noticeable, just a thin jagged line beginning to form across the ice blue sky, as though someone was drawing on it with a pencil. Sarah frowned, and wondered.

Far, far away, deep in the Great Forest of Alamore, in Caris Meriac, Oswain was woken from his sleep. He scratched his head. A nagging voice tugged at his mind. 'Go to the enchanted glade,' it insisted.

The King rose at once and made his way with haste to Elmere, the pool of visions, next to which glowed the famed Merestone that gave life to the forest. There, in the swirling waters of the pool and under the light of the star Elrilion, he saw a series of pictures: the sea, an island, children's faces and, standing on the island, a bloated stone idol. Then ice; cold, bleak ice everywhere. Oswain recognised the idol at once – a squat, ugly monstrosity that glowed with an ominous amber light. 'Shugob!' he whispered. He felt his hackles rise. If the Image was reviving, then what else was going on? The pool had given him a serious warning of trouble ahead. He would need to be ready.

* * *

The silence was broken and the heavens roared with a thunderous ripping sound that made Sarah clap her hands over her ears. With mounting horror she watched as the thin line became a jagged, black tear in the sky. Orange smoke began to pour through the hole. In seconds it took the form of giant fingers that started to rip the sky apart as though it were no more than a sheet of thin blue paper.

Sarah looked on helplessly as an enormous monster, ape-like and menacing, began to muscle through the black hole and into the world. At that same moment, the frozen wastes that stretched before her began to heave and to buckle. Suddenly, the ice exploded in a vast glittering geyser thrown hundreds of metres into the air by some incredible underground force.

Jets of flame spurted from the ground and from what looked like a sea of liquid fire there slowly rose a dazzling white pole on the top of which blazed a single star-like jewel of terrible beauty. Sarah watched in amazement as the monster reached down and grasped the shining sceptre in his great claw. As it did so, an evil grin creased its face, and in those malevolent gleaming eyes Sarah could see destruction, wars, riots, theft and violence, all kinds of greed and lawlessness, and lies without number.

Then somehow she was face to face with the monster. 'Join me,' it seemed to say. 'You cannot resist my power. Nobody can. Every living thing will bow to my will.'

'No! I won't,' cried the frightened girl.

'Yes, you will,' insisted the creature. The eyes full of evil pictures drew closer and closer to Sarah until she could see nothing else.

'Elmesh, help me!' she cried. 'Oswain, Oswain . . .'

'What is it, darling?' said a woman's voice.

Sarah jerked awake, her eyes wide with fear. Her mother, wrapped in a pink dressing gown, was gazing down at her with loving concern. A pool of yellow light from the landing told her that she was safe in her own bed.

'Oh, Mum,' she cried. 'I've just had the most awful dream. It was horrible!'

She began to sob and Mrs Brown put her arms around her daughter and held her close until she settled.

'Tell you what, why don't we go downstairs, have a nice cup of tea and talk about something else?' her mother suggested. 'Then you'll feel like going back to sleep again.'

Sarah smiled up at her mother's kindly face and nodded.

The next day she told her brothers, Peter and Andrew, about her dream. 'I'm sure Oswain needs us,' she concluded. 'Something terrible is going to happen to his world and we've got to stop it. I just know.'

'Hm, you may be right,' said Peter, who was the eldest. 'But there's nothing we can do about it, is there? I mean, I know we've been to the Great Forest before but we can't just go there whenever we like.'

'But you never know when it might happen,' said Andrew, who was full of excitement at the thought. 'If Sarah's dream is a message and not just one of her stupid ones, it could be quite soon!'

1

The Trapdoor

Nearly six weeks after Sarah's bad dream the three children were on holiday at Swanage in Dorset. A doctor friend had lent Mr and Mrs Brown a flat near Durlston Head so that Mrs Brown could convalesce after a nasty bout of 'flu.

Today, while their parents sunned themselves on the balcony, Peter, Sarah and Andrew were walking along the winding coastal path beyond the headland. Bright spring sun beamed down on them and the cliff-top gorse was celebrating Easter with a blaze of vivid yellow blossom. The air felt as fresh and sweet as clean laundry. It was the sort of day that made you feel good to be alive.

Ten-year-old Andrew, full of energy and eager to explore everything he could, had run on ahead with his dog, Tatters. His older brother and sister – Peter was just thirteen, and Sarah eleven – were taking things more slowly, stopping now and then to read the nature trail information about the birds which inhabited the cliffs. Peter had recently taken an interest in bird-watching and was hoping to get a pair of binoculars for his next birthday. Sarah wondered what it would be like to be a tern or an oyster-catcher.

They had just climbed out of the hollow by the Tilly Whim caves and were passing the lighthouse when they heard Tatters bark and their brother calling to them. Peter

spotted him waving from high up on the sloping grass-
land beyond the lighthouse buildings.

'Hey, come and see what I've found,' he shouted.

'What is it?' Peter called back.

'I'm not sure. It looks like some kind of trapdoor in the
ground.'

'What's so special about that?' Peter answered.

'Dunno, but it's got all sorts of strange carvings on it.
Could be an old way into the caves. Come and have a
look, anyway.'

'Oh, do we have to?' Sarah groaned. 'I'm quite happy
just walking along the path. I really don't want to get my
trainers messed up.'

'Same here, but he'll keep on and on if we don't,' said
her brother. 'Look, he's trying to pull it open, whatever it
is, and Tatters is going crazy. S'pose we'd better give him
a hand. Come on.'

When they reached Andrew, they found him tugging
away at a rusty iron ring fixed to an old and ornate
wooden door set in the ground. He grinned up at them.
'Help me pull it open, then,' he panted. 'It's too heavy for
me.'

'Are you sure we're meant to open it?' said Sarah. She
glanced up guiltily to see if anyone was watching them
from the lighthouse.

'It's probably only a sewer underneath,' Peter sniffed.
'What do you think, Tatters? I bet it stinks!'

The dog barked and ran about as though he was trying
to catch a fly. 'Hey, calm down, boy! It's OK,' Peter said.

Whatever Peter and Sarah's misgivings, Andrew's
enthusiasm won the day – after all, they agreed, it was an
unusual-looking door to find on a hillside. Curiosity

roused, they heaved together on the iron ring. At first nothing shifted and the children thought they might have to leave it. Then, with a painful squeaking of hinges, slowly the trapdoor lifted. Tatters growled and backed away.

'There, told you so. Just as I thought,' Peter exclaimed smugly. 'It's only water. Like I said, it's a sewer.'

At their feet lay the bright blue reflection of the sky. Andrew was disappointed.

Just then Peter noticed a fluttering bird reflected in the water. He glanced up expecting to see one of the many yellow-hammers that nested along the cliffs. To his surprise he couldn't see anything. It gave him an odd sensation, the feeling you get when something isn't quite right but you can't put your finger on it. He glanced down again and there, sure enough, he could still see the reflection of the bird in the water.

'That's odd,' he muttered.

'What is?' Sarah asked.

He explained and all three stooped down to get a closer look at the bird. They looked up at the sky again. It was still nowhere to be seen above them. Then they heard its call.

'You'd-better-come-quick. You'd-better-come-quick. You'd-better-come-quick – pleeese,' it seemed to say.

Tatters barked sharply and backed off even further.

How it happened nobody could afterwards quite explain, but the slight unease that Peter had sensed grew suddenly very strong and it was shared by his brother and sister. The hole seemed to expand before their eyes and they were all at once teetering on the edge of a sheer drop. Before anyone could utter another word, all three found themselves tumbling helplessly into the water.

Only it turned out not to be water after all. There was no expected splash, no cold soaking. In just a few moments, they were standing again on solid ground looking down at the trapdoor. But this time the twittering bird really was overhead, and there was no reflection in what they had thought was the water, and Tatters was nowhere to be seen.

Nobody spoke; the sensation of falling downwards only to find that they had fallen upwards – like falling right through the world and coming up on the other side – was all too much for their dazed minds. Peter felt queasy; he gulped and took a deep breath. Then, hardly daring, he risked a look round.

The countryside was quite different from the Dorset coastline. Gone were the sea and the lighthouse. Instead, they were in a valley and all around them rose high, wild, rocky hills. All three, to Peter's amazement, had lost their jeans, tee-shirts and trainers and were now clad in fur skins and boots. This was just as well because it was very cold and the ground was frozen hard, as though the morning frost had never thawed. From the look of the sun it was already the middle of the afternoon.

'You know what's happened?' he gasped. 'We're back in Oswain's world again! This has just got to be the Land Beyond the Far Places.'

Andrew's face broke into a grin. 'Wow, another adventure,' he cried. 'I knew it'd be worth opening that trapdoor.' He turned to his brother. 'What happened to the sewer, then, eh?'

Peter gave him a playful swipe.

'Oh, no,' Sarah wailed as her dream came flooding back to her. 'I'm not sure I'm going to like this.'

'Course you will,' Peter reassured her. 'It'll be great.'

Her brothers told her to stop worrying and cheer up. 'Anyway, you want to see Oswain and our friends again, don't you?' said Andrew. 'It'll be all right. You'll see.'

She smiled wanly and nodded. 'I guess so,' she sighed, and wondered why she always worried at the thought of coming danger but somehow was never really afraid once it arrived.

The yellow-hammer was still fluttering overhead. Its cry grew more shrill and insistent. *'You'd-better-come-quick. You'd-better-come-quick. You'd-better-come-quick – pleeese!'*

Sarah held out her finger and the bird fluttered down to rest. Cocking its head to one side it repeated its message, then flew up into the air again.

'I think it wants us to follow it,' said Peter.

The bird flew off up the frozen slope towards a small frost-rimmed thicket. The ground was rocky, as well as slippery, and the children had a tough time trying to keep up. By the time they reached the thicket, the bird was nowhere to be seen.

'Lost it,' said Andrew glumly.

Just then Sarah spotted an opening in some rocks that were half covered by the bushes. 'Perhaps it's gone in there,' she suggested.

Before her brothers could agree or disagree, the ground shook to the sound of a deep bellow which came from somewhere inside the crevice. It was followed by a shrill trilling noise like thousands of aspen leaves shivering in the breeze. Moments later, out from the crevice poured hundreds upon hundreds of black bats.

'Yuk!' cried Peter. All three backed off as fast as they could and watched as still more and more bats teemed from the rock until the sky overhead was black with them. The stench was horrible.

'Uggh! Let's get out of here,' cried Andrew. No one needed any further encouragement. They turned and ran back down the slope.

'What on earth caused that?' gasped Sarah as they came to a halt about two hundred metres away.

'No idea, but something nasty down there must have frightened them out,' said Peter. 'I've never seen anything like it.'

Further discussion was cut short by another loud roar. It was followed by a huge tongue of flame that leapt from the crevice causing all the surrounding shrubs to burst into flames. The children realised with a shock that if they had still been standing there they would surely have been burned alive. Incredulous, they watched as the fire crackled away, rapidly consuming the bushes and reducing them to blackened stumps.

'I don't think I like this very much,' muttered Peter. For a moment he wondered whether he should have taken more notice of his sister's misgivings. As the eldest, he often felt responsible for the other two.

'Me neither,' his brother agreed. 'Do you think that bird was trying to trap us?'

Before Peter could answer, Sarah called for their attention. 'Look!' she cried.

Their gaze followed her pointing finger. Bounding down the rock-strewn hillside, as agile as an antelope, was the wildest looking boy any of them had ever seen. He wore nothing but a tattered goatskin around his waist, and he ran barefooted. Wild-eyed and unkempt he raced towards the blaze.

He had obviously seen Peter, Sarah and Andrew and as he came to a halt between them and the diminishing flames he began to wave his arms wildly to warn them off. 'Tergan! Tergan!' he cried in a harsh voice. 'Go away. Not safe.'

With that he was off, back the way that he had come.

'Come on!' cried Peter. 'We've got to follow him.'

At once, all three hared up the hillside after the strange-looking boy.

Higher and higher they clambered until their legs were buckling with the effort, but still the boy ran on, bounding over the icy rocks as though they scarcely existed and never once stopping to wait for them.

It may have been something in the air, but after a while each of the children began to feel light-headed. The world up here was strange and slightly unreal and the only sounds they could hear were those of their panting lungs and the occasional scrunch of their boots on loose rock. In spite of the heat caused by their exertions, they found it much colder on what they now appreciated was the side of a mountain, and they were glad of the warm furs. The wild boy, although lacking adequate clothing, did not seem to mind the cold one little bit.

No one knew how long they climbed nor how high they had come, yet still they could not catch up with the fleeing figure of the boy. Soon the day wore out and it began to grow dark; it became harder and harder to see and when they had almost reached what looked like the summit they lost sight of him altogether. Peter came to a halt and waited until his brother and sister caught up with him. For a while nobody could say a word as they gasped and panted for breath.

'Well, now what?' Andrew asked once he had regained his voice.

'Dunno,' his brother answered. 'This is a weird start to an adventure, if you ask me!'

Sarah looked around. In the fading light she could just make out a silvery sea far below. From the way it curved around the bays it looked very much as though they might be on an island, but she couldn't be sure. Maybe they could tell from the summit.

'Well, since we've come this far, we might as well go to the top,' she suggested.

They agreed and were soon clambering over the last broken rocks that marked the peak. But the sight that met their eyes was as unexpected as everything else so far. The summit turned out to be a ridge that fell away into a steep, snow-covered crater. In the pink glow of sunset they could just make out that they were standing on the rim of a vast volcano, the inside slopes of which were for some reason completely covered in thick ice. Far down below they could see faint lights twinkling in the gloom.

'Wow . . .,' began Andrew. But before anyone could comment on this strange scene they were startled by the sound of a harsh voice.

'Strib 341 commands you. Stop where you are!'

The children whirled round and nearly jumped out of their skins. Sarah gasped, while Peter and Andrew's mouths dropped open in sheer disbelief. What they saw was so unexpected that they could scarcely believe their eyes. And it was coming straight towards them.

2
Lord Yarx

The speaker was a simply enormous penguin. He was as tall as Peter and armed with a long glinting spear, that looked as though it was made of ice, and which he was brandishing in their direction. Nor was he alone. Accompanying him were over a dozen others, each also carrying a spear. They moved swiftly to surround the children.

'Do you think they're friendly?' Andrew asked doubtfully.

'Doesn't exactly look like it, does it?' his brother retorted, staring at the penguins and their menacing spears. Maybe it was his imagination, but the edges of their bills looked decidedly blood-red in the dying daylight.

'Perhaps it's like when we first came into the Great Forest. You know, when the forest-folk thought we were on Hagbane's side,' Sarah suggested. 'I've always thought penguins were quite cute,' she added hopefully, but one look at the penguins' expressions was enough to convince her that in this case it was unlikely. Not that they were angry. It was something odd about their eyes which disturbed her.

'You will come with us. This is a Strib order which must be obeyed,' commanded the first penguin, who was clearly in charge. Peter noticed that he had a white bar on one flipper.

'Supposing we don't?' ventured Andrew.

'Truants will be severely punished and expelled if they do not return at once. This is a Strib order which must be obeyed.'

'Huh?'

'We'd better do as they say,' Peter muttered, eyeing the penguins, who were now crowding around them and leaving no way of escape. He nodded to their leader. 'We'll come with you,' he said.

Closely shadowed by their captors they were driven along a narrow path that wound between the shattered rocks rimming the volcano. After about five minutes' walk the path brought them once again to the very brink of the precipice. There, to their amazement, they were confronted by a vast glass-smooth slope of ice, the bottom of which disappeared into the gloom all of five hundred metres below. Without hesitation, the first three penguins leapt over the top and slithered at great speed down the slope and into the darkness.

'You will follow them. This is a Strib order which must obeyed,' commanded the leader.

'I can't do that!' Sarah wailed.

'You must be joking,' Peter exclaimed.

'No way!' said Andrew.

In spite of their protests, the penguins prodded them with their spears until they were standing right on the icy brink, trying to pluck up the courage to jump, and dearly wishing that they were somewhere else.

Peter made up his mind. 'Let's all go together,' he said. 'Come on, hold hands. If they can do it, I guess so can we.' He grabbed their hands. 'Come on, one, two, three – yaaaahh!'

With cries of alarm, all three leapt together.

The first part of the slope was so steep that it felt as if they were simply falling over the side of a mountain. Then the ice began to level off and their descent turned out to be an utterly breathtaking slide that was like being on the longest, smoothest sleigh run in the world. In spite of the danger by the time they had reached the lower slopes, all three were shouting and whooping and squealing with excitement.

'How do we stop?' Andrew yelled.

'Don't know!' cried Peter. 'But it must be all right otherwise the penguins wouldn't have done it.'

'Maybe they're kamikaze penguins!' Andrew retorted.

However, at last the slope levelled out and without harm they slid to a halt. Shaking slightly, they staggered to their feet.

'Want to make a run for it, Pete?' said Andrew.

His brother shook his head. They were surrounded by yet more spear-carrying penguins and, a few moments later, the rest of the party that had arrested them slithered alongside.

'You will come with us,' said the captain. 'This is a . . .'

'I know,' Peter sighed. 'A Strib order which must be obeyed. Come on, everyone!'

It wasn't easy walking on the ice and they slid rather than walked through the gloom as the penguins ushered them towards the twinkling lights which they had seen from the top.

They found themselves in an amazing world. All around, the walls of the volcano rose like a huge black curtain that shut them off from the outside world. They had to crane their necks to see the last remnants of the

dying day far above. Already the first stars were beginning to appear. But down here there was plenty of light.
It came, they discovered, from large crystals set at regular
intervals in pillars of ice, so that they seemed to be
walking along a well-marked highway which sparkled
beneath their feet.

Ahead stood a massive dome-shaped igloo which
glowed bluish white in the crystal lamplight. Peter
noticed that there were other similar but smaller igloos
dotted about the plain. He also thought he could see at
some distance a large crystalline pyramid that glowed
with a hidden fire of its own, but he had no idea what it
was.

If it were not for the danger they were in, Sarah would
have said it was all rather pretty, a bit like a winter fairyland at night. She said as much to Andrew.

'Fairyland? More like furry land!' he retorted. 'And
they all smell of stale fish. Furry, fishy land, that's what it
is!'

They were marched into a tunnel. It led them inside the
largest of the igloos where everything was brightly lit by
yet more crystals set in the walls. The three children gazed
around in wonder. Who could have built such a vast
cavern of ice? Peter hoped that they were about to meet
whoever was really in charge. Then he could ask what it
was all about.

Their captors brought them at last to face a high dais
carved from ice where they were instructed to wait. Two
minutes later three very large emperor penguins emerged
from a doorway behind the dais. Each one wore a gown
of the kind that you sometimes see university lecturers
wearing on special occasions. Sarah thought they looked

rather grand with their yellow and red markings. These, as the children were soon to find out, were the leaders, and they were called Strats. All the other ordinary penguins were called Stribs and were under the command of captains who gave 'Strib orders'.

The centre Strat gazed down coldly upon the captives. When he spoke, his voice was rasping.

'Your names, truants?'

'It is a Strat order,' began the captain of the guard when they hesitated.

'A Strat order, eh?' said Andrew cheekily. 'It must be important, then! Is that different from a Strib order? And what does he mean, truants?'

'Answer!' screeched the emperor penguin.

'Why should we?' Andrew retorted.

'Answer!'

'It is a Strat order which must be obeyed.'

'This is going to get boring,' said Sarah.

'You're right,' sighed Peter. 'Oh well, can't do any harm, I suppose. I'm Peter,' he answered.

'And I'm Sarah.'

'Me, I'm Andrew, and I want to know what we're doing here and who you are. What are your names?' he demanded. His voice echoed off the walls. 'You've no right to hold us here.' He wished that Tatters was with them; that would show them who was boss!

The Strat – who was obviously the chief – held the lapels of his gown with his flippers and addressed them importantly.

'I am Lord Yarx. This you would have learned soon enough if you had not sought to escape. To me, together with my comrade Strats, Senators Raaz and Kig, is granted the privilege of leading you in serving the Great Purpose. And since you have the arrogance to be here before the proper time you will begin to serve that purpose at once!'

'I'm afraid we don't know what you're talking about,' said Peter, stepping forward. 'What do you mean, escaped? Escaped from where? We want to know what's going on first of all. We aren't just going to join you and some Great Purpose without knowing what it is. And . . . and you had better tell us whether you are servants of Elmesh or not,' he added as an afterthought.

The emperor penguin who had seated himself on Yarx's right hand side rose angrily. 'Elmesh! What is that?' he demanded, wagging a flipper in Peter's direction. 'There is no such thing as Elmesh!'

'That does it, then!' cried Sarah hotly. 'If you're so stupid as not to believe in him, then we're certainly not going to join any so-called Great Purpose of yours! So there!'

'You will join us,' continued Lord Yarx. 'You have no choice. There is nothing else. Progress must be served.'

'No, we won't. Why should we?' Andrew exclaimed. 'What right have you got to tell us what to do?'

'There is no other way of thinking or behaving,' answered the third emperor penguin. 'This is the only way forward. You must take it, as must we all. Is that not obvious? You should have learned this by now.'

'You haven't yet told us what this Great Purpose is,' Peter replied carefully.

'You will learn of it soon enough, when your education is complete. Such questions must not be asked too soon,' the penguin answered. 'Now, as punishment for playing truant you will be kept here and put to hard labour tomorrow. That is all.'

Peter made to protest but Andrew nudged him.

'Best go along with it, Pete. We can't make a break for it at the moment, anyway. And we might learn a bit more about what's really going on here. I reckon it's as fishy as they smell!'

His brother nodded.

'Very well, we'll do as you say. For the moment,' he added.

'Of course you will,' said Yarx. 'There is no other possible way!'

'You will follow me,' said the captain. 'This is a Strib order . . .'

'We know,' chorused the children, 'which must be obeyed!'

They were led along another corridor made of ice which eventually opened out into a cavern that was partitioned off into many doorless cubicles. Here hundreds of penguins were sleeping in neat rows, five penguins to each cubicle. The children were marched down the cavern's length until they came to an empty cell against the far wall.

'This is where you will sleep,' commanded the penguin.

'What, no bedding or pillows?' cried Sarah. 'And it's so cold here.'

'You will sleep here,' repeated the penguin.

'What about food and water?' said Andrew. 'I'm hungry.'

'No more food is served until dawn,' answered the penguin. 'You will now sleep. This is a Strib order which must be obeyed.'

He waited while they lay down in a row on the floor, then departed.

'Thank goodness we've got warm clothes on,' said Peter. 'At least I don't feel too cold at the moment.'

'Nor me,' said Andrew. 'But we can hardly live long in this place. It's all very well for penguins, but we're not exactly designed for sleeping on beds of ice, are we?'

'I wish Oswain and Loriana were here,' sighed Sarah. 'They would get us out of this.' She sat up. 'You know, I was really angry when that penguin said Elmesh didn't exist.'

'Me too,' said Andrew. 'Of all the cheek!'

'How are we going to escape, Peter?' his sister asked. 'There's no way we can climb back up that slope. There has to be another way though. After all, the penguins got to the top somehow.'

'Hmm, I agree,' nodded her brother. 'We'll have to try tomorrow, though. Can't do anything in the dark. Better see if we can get some sleep, I suppose.'

It wasn't easy sleeping on the hard, cold ice and even though they arranged themselves in a circle so that their heads rested on each other's stomachs they slept only fitfully.

After what seemed to be no more than two or three hours, all three were jerked awake by a sound like a klaxon horn which echoed around the cavern.

'What on earth was that?' exclaimed Peter.

'Rising bell, I think,' replied Andrew ruefully. 'Come on, Sarah. Breakfast time!'

The children staggered to their feet, feeling very stiff and aching all over.

'Ugh, where's the grub?' groaned Andrew as he stretched. 'I feel awful!'

'You look it,' Peter retorted with a laugh.

They were interrupted by a voice booming through the cavern. 'Attention. All Stribs will assemble for breakfast!'

'Hurray!' Andrew exclaimed. 'Come on, let's be Stribs for a little while.'

He was to be very disappointed. They stumbled from their cubicle to find hundreds of penguins already neatly lined up. At another command they waddled into the main cavern where, in the middle of the floor, lay a large pile of fish and a pool of water. In an orderly fashion each penguin took one fish and bent briefly to drink.

'Ugh, raw fish!' exclaimed Sarah. 'I'm not eating that! Isn't there anything else?'

'Eat,' commanded a penguin guard.

Peter rounded on him angrily. 'Look, this may be all right for you but we don't eat raw fish for breakfast.'

'No, we want cornflakes or muesli,' said Andrew. 'And eggs and bacon, and toast and marmalade,' he added as an afterthought.

'You eat this or you do not eat,' replied the penguin.

'I couldn't,' said Sarah.

'Nor me,' added Peter.

'I don't even think I could,' murmured Andrew, eyeing the fast diminishing heap of fish.

'You will now go to be educated,' ordered a voice. 'Line up all Stribs.'

'We've just got to get out of here,' muttered Peter as they shuffled to obey.

'Yeah, and as soon as possible, or we'll die of starvation!' said Andrew.

Just then Sarah gave a gasp.

'What is it, Sarah?' Peter asked.

'Don't look now, but up there on the right there's a high ledge. I think I can see that wild boy, and he's watching us!'

3

Prisoners of the Penguins

'Whose side do you reckon he's on?' whispered Andrew.

'Dunno,' his brother replied. 'But we'd better not take any chances. Let's face it, it's all because we followed him that we got caught by these penguins in the first place.'

'I wish I knew what was really going on,' Sarah sighed. 'I mean, whoever heard of penguins called Stribs and Strats? And what's this Great Purpose of theirs?'

Her questions were interrupted by the appearance of one of the Strib captains.

'Silence!' he commanded. 'It is not permitted for you to speak before assembly.'

All the penguins were lined up in a single column, each one staring straight ahead. The children were made to join them. For a moment Andrew imagined they were a row of dominoes and had to resist the urge to push one of them over to see if the whole line would fall down. His thoughts were broken by another Strib command. At this the penguins began to waddle towards a tunnel leading out of the great dome.

Peter stole a quick glance up to the ledge, but the wild boy was nowhere to be seen. Was he a friend or a foe, he wondered?

The tunnel was not very long and soon the children found they were entering another dome, smaller than the one they had left but lit in the same manner. The penguins moved without fuss into orderly ranks, standing in blocks of twenty facing a raised platform carved out of ice. It seemed that the Stribs with white bands were the captains, and it was they who supervised the proceedings. Threatened by their spears, Peter, Sarah and Andrew stood in one of the ranks at the back.

'All hail to Lord Yarx!' commanded one of the captains, breaking the silence.

The penguins raised their flippers and began to clap loudly as they chanted. 'All hail to Lord Yarx.' The children steadfastly refused to join in.

'I'm not cheering some nutty penguin,' muttered Andrew.

'Nor me,' said Sarah.

Yarx entered the dome and ceremoniously mounted the platform, accompanied by his senators, Raaz and Kig. He raised a flipper. At once the penguins were silent. A mysterious force seemed to come from his eyes and Sarah was now convinced that the penguins were all under some kind of spell. Why else would they act like this?

Yarx began to speak. 'Today, loyal Stribs, is another step forward in the Great Purpose. You are privileged to serve the call of the Prophetess of the stars. All is foretold and already the signs are in the heavens. They herald the dawn of a new age. By knowledge, by skill and craft in unlocking secret wisdom, we shall become the rulers of our own destiny.

'The age of the old superstitions is over, finished are the unchanging rules of life. No longer will we be shackled to the past. Freedom! I promise you freedom, and power to be the masters of your own future!'

At this all the penguins began to clap loudly and to

cheer with loud cries. Yarx looked around and his face was smug.

'What a load of old garbage!' Andrew whispered.

'Learn, and work well, for this is an opportunity not to be lost. To your labours!' cried Yarx.

Whereupon, under the command of the captains, the penguins marched off in different directions. As they did so the children heard the sound of a stringed instrument like a harp and the penguins began to chant to its rhythm.

> 'When ice and fire shall meet,
> Then earth and sky be one;
> The Lord beneath the earth
> Shall join the Lord above;
> So speaks the Prophetess;
> For us the wealth and fame!'

'What a weird song,' said Andrew. 'I wonder what it means?'

'Haven't a clue,' Peter replied. 'But I'm not singing it, that's for sure!'

'Nor me,' added Sarah. 'I don't know what this is all about, but I reckon these Stribs and Strats are up to no good at all. And where do you think that music is coming from?'

Before they could discuss further, one of the Strib captains came across with a posse of armed penguins. He addressed Peter.

'As punishment for your truancy you will be put to work digging the Great Channel,' he said. 'Follow me.'

'Wait!' The command came from Senator Raaz. 'Bring the truants before me.'

The Stribs obeyed, their spears urging the reluctant trio forward. The Strat eyed them keenly.

'These two will dig,' he said, indicating Peter and Andrew. 'But this one will work for me.' He pointed at Sarah. 'Take them away!'

Peter tried to argue but soon discovered that the spears were sharp and that the penguins knew how to use them. He and his brother were hustled out of the cave, leaving Sarah in the charge of Senator Raaz.

Outside, the scenery was as breathtaking as an alpine landscape. The icy cliffs towering around them glistened and sparkled where they were struck by the bright beams of the morning sun, or else were lost in translucent blue shadows and drifts of pale mist. The air smelt crisp, and reminded Peter of a skiing holiday he had been on with his school.

Now that it was daytime, the boys could get a better picture of where they were. They appeared to be on the floor of an extinct volcano which Peter estimated to be probably over a mile in diameter – Andrew said one and a half kilometres, but neither of them really knew. The walls rose steeply on all sides and, as they had discovered already, were covered in thick ice. Climbing them would be extremely difficult and probably impossible without the right equipment, Peter judged.

The penguin dwellings consisted of a number of igloos joined by tunnels of ice, and standing at a distance from them was the tall crystalline pyramid that glowed, not just in the sun, but from something hidden inside it. But the boys couldn't make out what this was.

They were provided with odd-looking shovels and told to work with other penguins who were digging a deep channel. It appeared to start at the pyramid and to run across the frozen plain to a destination unknown. As they dug the Stribs continued their chant to the sound of the harp playing.

> 'When ice and fire shall meet,
> Then earth and sky be one;
> The Lord beneath the earth
> Shall join the Lord above;
> So speaks the Prophetess;
> For us the wealth and fame!'

'I wonder what's in that pyramid and what this trench is for,' said Peter.

'I wonder what Sarah's doing,' answered his brother. He hoped she was all right.

'Start digging,' commanded a captain when he saw them talking. 'This is a Strib order which must be obeyed.'

They took a look at their strange shovels. The tools had a narrow curved blade on one side with a steel hook on the other. The penguins used the hook as a gouge and then shovelled the broken ice with the blade. The shaft contained two sockets clearly designed to fit penguin flippers but quite unsuitable for human hands.

'We can't use these,' Peter protested.

'Silence! It is a Strib order which must be obeyed.'

Peter huffed, and he and his brother began to make a half-hearted effort to use their shovels, if only to get the captain off their backs.

Sarah, meanwhile, was taken to one of the smaller igloos. She found herself in a class of about fifty penguins presided over by Raaz himself. He ordered her to a bench carved from ice upon which stood crystals of many different sizes and shapes, along with beakers of coloured liquids, none of which she recognised. The penguins were working at similar benches around her and at first she thought it was a chemistry class. However, it soon became clear that this was something different. She watched as the Stribs began mixing the crystals and liquids in bowls before bringing them to Raaz. He then placed their work in the middle of a pyramid-shaped frame made of silver.

Then Senator Raaz moaned a strange chant which Sarah didn't like at all. As he did so, the pyramid began to turn and to glow orange, with a crackling noise like static electricity. Sometimes a few sparks would fly and the crystals begin to glow. At this everyone would be very pleased. But most of the time nothing happened and the Strib was sent away to try again.

Those whose mixtures sparked were separated from the rest to concentrate on their experiments. All of them were making notes in some kind of hieroglyphics made by dabbing black ink onto ice tablets with their flippers.

Sarah didn't want to do any of this but they kept saying it was a Strat order which must be obeyed, and in the end, just to keep them quiet, she began to mess about with the crystals and liquids. She wished she was somewhere else, preferably in the Great Forest with Oswain and his friends.

Then one of the Strib captains came and took what she was doing across to the pyramid. Raaz began his chant and to Sarah's amazement and dismay her careless effort sparked and crackled more than all the rest. The Strat was delighted and Sarah was ushered into his presence.

'You will show us how you did this,' he croaked. 'It is of vital importance to the Great Purpose.'

'But I don't know,' began Sarah. 'I was just messing about.'

'Foolish pupil! Where are your notes?' exclaimed the Strat.

'I haven't got any,' she explained. 'I don't even . . .'

'You must work until you can do this again. Over there!'

Sarah made to protest but realised she was getting nowhere and the armed Strib allowed no argument. Sulkily, she returned and began to scribble with the ink by dipping her finger in it. She began by writing, *Stribs and Strats are rubbish!* and didn't care if they could understand it or not.

All day Sarah stood at the bench wishing her crystals hadn't worked. From time to time they wanted to see what was going on. She kept saying it was a very long formula and she was trying hard to remember it. Every so often they would try her experiment but it never worked again and they became more and more cross with her. It was a hateful place, she decided, and she just wished she and her brothers could find a way to escape. She was also feeling very hungry.

By the end of the day she was crying and beginning to wish something would work, simply to stop them nagging at her. When the other Stribs were ordered to end their work for the day she was kept there and, surrounded by armed Stribs, was made to keep on mixing crystals and liquids, while they wrote down everything as she went. She felt weak, tired, and utterly wretched, and her tummy hurt for lack of food.

Peter and Andrew were greatly relieved when they were allowed to stop for the day. They too felt weak from not

having eaten and their heads were ringing with the con-
stant chanting. More raw fish had been brought out at
lunch time but, hungry as they were, neither could face
the thought of eating it.

'Whew, we can't go on like this, Pete,' gasped Andrew.
'We'll be dead at this rate.'

'Somehow I don't think they care whether anyone dies
or not,' his brother replied, as he inspected his chafed
hands. 'I mean they really are weird, aren't they? Sort of
hypnotised, I'd say. They don't seem to care about us, or
even one another.'

'Do you think they're robots – you know, androids, or
should I say penguinoids?' asked Andrew.

'No, I don't think so, otherwise they wouldn't need to
eat fish, would they? And I saw one of them cut his flipper
earlier today.'

'Then what's happened to them and why are they here?'

'And where did they get these shovels and stuff?'

These were questions which neither could answer.
Wearily they trudged back to the main igloo, from where
they were escorted to their icy cell. Sarah was nowhere to
be seen.

'Where's our sister?' demanded Peter.

'She still works. It is a supreme Strat order and cannot
be disobeyed,' replied the captain.

'Stuff that!' exclaimed Peter hotly. 'We're going to find
her!'

They were met at once by a hostile array of ice spears
and one of them stabbed the back of Peter's hand,
drawing blood.

'What are we going to do, Pete?' cried Andrew in exas-
peration. 'This is ridiculous!'

'I dunno,' muttered his brother as he sucked his hand. 'Let's lie down and pretend to sleep. Perhaps the guards will go away.'

They curled up on the frozen floor, and were so exhausted that in spite of their efforts to keep awake, sleep quickly overtook both of them. The guards moved away.

Peter was roused suddenly by something hitting him. He sat up and rubbed his eyes. Again, a small object struck him. He turned to Andrew but his brother was still dozing. A third missile hit him and he saw that it was a small stone. He nudged his brother.

'Eh, wassermarra? Is Sarah back?' yawned Andrew.

'No, somebody's throwing stones.'

'Well, throw them back,' he groaned.

But Peter was on his feet.

Then he saw him. The wild boy was beckoning to him, holding a finger over his lips to warn them not to speak.

'Come on, Andrew,' Peter muttered. 'It's that wild boy. We're gonna have to take the risk. Let's follow him.'

So, the two brothers, without their sister, and not knowing whether or not they could trust the wild boy, slipped from their cell and crept off into the unknown.

4

The Frozen Lake

Many miles to the north, it was springtime in the Great Forest and everywhere the trees were sporting their fresh green finery above thick carpets of bluebells and scattered daffodils. Birds were busily and noisily building their nests, and the woodland glades were a buzz of activity as the forest-folk took full advantage of the fine weather.

In spite of this, all was not well. Oswain and the Ice Maiden, Loriana, were staring silently southwards over Lake Coramere. Neither smiled at the sight, for from where they stood it looked like a scene from a winter postcard. Thick hoarfrost covered the land with white as far as the eye could see. No buds had opened, no flowers were blooming, there wasn't an animal in sight. Lake Coramere was frozen solid. Despite the warm sunshine, spring had failed to come to the southern part of the kingdom. Indeed, the bitter cold was actually spreading steadily northwards, and had been doing so for several weeks.

The forest-folk who dwelt in the south were the first to bring the news, for they were migrating north in great numbers to escape the cold. Oswain and the Ice Maiden had journeyed to the southern part of the forest to take a look for themselves.

'This isn't simply a late spring,' murmured Loriana. 'There's something wrong. This part of the forest never sees the frost, not even in winter.'

Oswain agreed. 'We are not used to it. If this cold continues northwards the forest as we know it will die and all the forest-folk with it.'

'You were warned when you looked into the enchanted pool.'

'Yes. Elmere reveals visions and sometimes mysterious ones, but it never lies,' he answered.

'We must do something about it, Oswain, and as soon as possible.'

'I agree, but I honestly don't know where to start.'

They were just turning to go when Oswain's keen eyes spotted a dark speck in the distance. He shaded his eyes against the sun. It soon became apparent that a large bird was winging towards them.

'It's a pelican,' exclaimed the Ice Maiden. 'I wonder what it's doing so far from the sea?'

It was not long before her question was answered. The bird was coming in to land, but in the most ungainly manner you could ever imagine. It was swerving from side to side, twisting and turning, bucking and rolling, its wings flapping furiously in spite of the calm air, until at last it belly-flopped on the frozen lake with a loud squawk. From there it slid and spun across the surface before finally slithering to a crumpled and rather bedraggled halt at the feet of the two companions. They found themselves gazing down at a battered, moth-eaten old pelican with a pair of spectacles hanging lopsidedly around its neck.

'Flip me, what kind of landing was that?' came a voice from its beak.

'I can't help it. I can't see a thing with these glasses all frosted up. You try landing on ice and see how you like it!'

came another voice. 'Anyway, you kept moving like loose ballast. Quite upset my airworthiness, you did.'

'Oh, never mind. Just let me out. I've had enough of being cooped up in here.'

'Nothing but complaints all day long. That's all I get,' sighed the pelican. 'Go on, out you get then!'

The pelican opened its pouched beak, and out stumbled a pompous-looking puffin wearing a bowler hat and carrying a rolled-up umbrella tucked under his wing. On spotting Oswain and Loriana he at once drew himself up to his full height, puffed out his chest and with a loud 'Hrumph', addressed them in the most official-sounding voice he could muster.

'Would you by any chance, sir, be Oswain, King of the Great Forest of Alamore, Son of the High King of the West, and you madam, his lady consort, Loriana, the Ice Maiden?'

'Why, yes!' they said, glancing at each other and laughing.

'Good, then I am addressing the correct personages,' he replied. He removed his bowler hat.

'Thank goodness for that!' gasped the pelican who had by now struggled to his feet. 'Wheezer's the name, your Majesties,' he added. 'At your service.' He bowed, and promptly slipped flat on his face.

'Good morning, Mr Wheezer,' laughed Oswain. 'And your name, sir?' he asked, turning to the puffin.

'I, sir, am Horatio the Third, also at your service.'

'And what brings you to these parts?' enquired the Ice Maiden.

'We have an urgent message,' Wheezer replied promptly.

'An important message,' corrected the puffin.

Oswain leaned back against a tree. 'Urgent messages which are also important should be given our full attention,' he said. 'We are eager to hear what you have to tell us!'

'I'll do the talking,' declared Horatio the Third, addressing his companion. He turned to Oswain and Loriana, paused for effect, then clearing his throat with another 'Hrumph' he began.

'I am instructed to inform your Majesties of news of the gravest kind. You see before you the approaching ice and wonder why it is so.' He gestured with his umbrella. 'I will tell you.' He paused and looked at them severely. Then, in almost a whisper, he announced, 'The penguins have stolen the South Pole!'

'What?' gasped the Ice Maiden.

'Where did you obtain this information?' Oswain demanded, the humour vanishing from his eyes.

'We've been following them for days,' wheezed the pelican. 'It's been awful.'

'But how did you know?' Oswain pressed.

'Because a great white eagle told us, or rather, me,' answered the puffin.

'Arca?' queried Loriana.

'That was his name, I do believe.'

'Then why didn't he come himself?'

'He said he's rallying support,' Horatio replied. 'Said something about it heralding terrible tragedy for the whole world if what they're trying to do really comes to pass.'

'Did he say what that was' asked the Ice Maiden.

'Well actually, no, he didn't, as far as I can recall. He

didn't look the sort that the likes of puffins argue with, so I didn't press him. He told me to investigate and then to seek you out as soon as I could.' He glanced in Wheezer's direction. 'The journey was too great for me so I enlisted the help of this pelican. On the King's business, if you will pardon me, sir. Together we scanned the ocean until we saw the truth of the eagle's words for ourselves.'

For the next hour Oswain and Ice Maiden quizzed the two unlikely messengers. They learned that thousands of penguins had, for reasons unknown and with an uncanny power, stolen the South Pole and begun to march northwards. Wherever they had taken it everything for hundreds of miles around had frozen solid, so that they had been able to travel across the sea on a single vast sheet of ice.

Such was the terrible power of the South Pole that the penguins carrying it died after a day or two and many hundreds had fallen on the journey.

'They were led by three emperor penguins who seemed to exert a terrifying control over the rest,' Wheezer explained. 'In spite of the death toll, others always took the place of those who had fallen.'

'Anything else?' Oswain demanded.

'Well, there did seem to be an orange haze over them,' croaked Wheezer. 'I thought it was my glasses at first, but it wasn't. Even at night you could still see it. Kind of glowing, it was.'

'And where are they now?' asked the Ice Maiden.

'On the island of Aethius,' the puffin replied.

'That's about three hundred miles from here,' Oswain observed. 'Then this much is clear. We must journey to the island as soon as possible. There is little doubt that this is the cause of the frost which is destroying our springtime.'

'But how, sir, will you take your journey? The sea is frozen all the way there, and you cannot use a boat,' said Horatio.

'And what of the river that leads from this lake?' asked Oswain.

'That's frozen, too.'

Oswain thought for a moment. Then his face brightened. 'Good, then we will build an ice yacht suitable for such a journey!'

* * *

Back in the heart of the Great Forest where Oswain's chief advisor and long-time friend, the aged badger Lord Trotter dwelt, Oswain called a meeting of the Council.

Present were the badgers, Lord and Lady Trotter, Stiggle the weasel who was commander-in-chief, and the three mice, Fumble, Mumble and Grumble. They all assembled with Oswain and the Ice Maiden in Trotter's cottage.

'What on earth has made them do it?' Stiggle asked. 'I know very little about such creatures but I thought that penguins were peaceful.'

'So they are, in normal circumstances,' the Ice Maiden answered. 'We must assume that something, or someone, has affected their behaviour.'

'I will hazard a guess; it is Shugob the Devourer,' said Oswain. His eyes narrowed.

'It is a hateful name and a hateful being,' growled Trotter with distaste. 'Do you think this is another attempt on Caris Meriac, Oswain?'

The King nodded thoughtfully. 'Possibly. It was a long time ago.'

'We mice know little of those days,' said Grumble. 'We only know that it was the beginning of the Great Unrest.'

Oswain shifted his gaze to the mouse. 'It was indeed, and both Trotter's father, Rufus the Strong and my father, King Argil, played a great part in the defeat of Shugob when he last sought to invade our world.'

'It is a noble tale that should be told in full,' said Trotter. 'But we do not have the time now. The forest is freezing over and we need urgent action.'

'This island, what do you know of it?' asked Stiggle.

'From what I am told it is a strange place,' Oswain replied. 'It is a volcanic island that from time to time rises from the ocean and later sinks again.'

'Legend has it that some of the evils of the Great Unrest fled there upon their defeat, but that they were all drowned,' said the Ice Maiden.

'That was not all. The greatest treasure in all Caris Meriac was stolen and is believed to have been taken there and lost in the destruction,' Trotter added.

'Wawasthat?' asked Mumble.

'It was a rare thing indeed. A book. The Tale of the Seven Rainbows. Some also call it the Book of Truth,' Trotter replied. 'How I would love to have seen it for myself. It is said that it contained the greatest of the works and wisdom of Elmesh.'

'It has long gone, sad to say, and the world is poorer for the fact,' Oswain added.

'It may be only chance that the penguins have gone to Aethius,' said Fumble. 'Or there may be more to it. It needs investigating, that's for sure.'

On that the whole Council was agreed and Trotter summed up the proceedings with his recommendation. 'I suggest that Oswain and Loriana, together with Wheezer and Horatio, make the journey,' he said. 'We have a crisis in the forest because of the numbers of refugees from the south. If we are not careful soon even forest-folk will be quarrelling for space.'

'We also need to send word to Elmar,' said Oswain. 'My parents may be old but they will remember the past and may have some wisdom to offer. My sister, Princess Alena, too.'

'I would like to make that journey myself,' said Mrs Trotter from where she sat in her favourite armchair. Trotter looked at his wife in amazement. 'Well, I've never been there,' she explained.

Oswain laughed. 'An excellent idea,' he said. 'It is high time that you visited my home city, Lady Trotter! And Stiggle shall accompany you on the way. Though the road is safe it is seldom good to travel alone.'

'Then I'll pack my things,' she answered. 'You will be needed here, my dear,' she said to her bemused husband.

The next few days were marked by a great flurry of activity as many different animals, but beavers especially, prepared to accompany Oswain to the lake. Others had been collecting silk from the silkworms and weaving it into strong cords and sailcloth. Once at the lakeside they intended to build the ice yacht that would carry their leaders to the mysterious island of Aethius. Even old

Trotter, having seen his wife and Stiggle on their way, decided he would make the journey to the lake and see them off.

It took two days' travel to return to the head of Lake Coramere and another three days of furious activity and grim determination to build a craft which would travel over the ice. Even during that time the cold had advanced northwards and flowers and new leaves once so fresh, now hung dead, scorched black by the frost.

At last the great log-sleigh was finished, and a fine sight it was, resting its runners on the frozen lake, well-laden with provisions and ready for the journey. A large sail hung limply from its single mast and a tiller edged with steel teeth was set to steer it. They named the craft *The Felstar*.

The Ice Maiden had not yet joined them because she had other business to attend to in the north. Oswain knew she had gone to the mountains and now waited expectantly for her return.

The day came, bright and clear, when they were to set off. All the animals who had worked so hard gathered on the shore of the lake to wave goodbye.

'But where is Loriana?' asked Trotter.

Oswain smiled and looked up. 'Here she comes!' he cried.

To the wonder of all who watched, the Ice Maiden came floating towards them through the air, clad in a flowing garment of purest silver-blue silk. Beneath her feet and bearing her along was a cluster of glittering spangles, dancing brightly in the sunlight. The air was filled with a sweet bell-like music.

The forest-folk heralded her arrival with shouts and cheers, and a round of applause.

'Greetings,' she called with a smile and pointed to the spangles. 'And look, the Naida have come, too!'

She descended by the lakeside and rushed to embrace Oswain. The Naida hovered over the lake at a distance lest their presence should cause the forest-folk to feel drowsy, as was often the case with those unused to their powers.

In a short while the final preparations were complete and Oswain and Loriana made ready to board their craft.

'My friend, may Elmesh go with you,' said Trotter, taking Oswain's hand.

The Ice Maiden bent and kissed him. 'And you take good care of yourselves,' she said.

'Our prayers for your success go with you,' the badger replied. He looked up again at the sky. It was decidedly chillier, though the sun still shone. 'And may you indeed have success,' he said with feeling.

Oswain and Loriana climbed aboard the ice-yacht. They were accompanied by Wheezer who took his perch on the prow. Horatio the Third said he had done enough travelling with the pelican for the time being and chose in the end to remain with the forest-folk. Oswain, wearing a heavy woollen cloak, prepared to raise the sail. The Ice Maiden, who neither feared nor felt the cold, revelled in the climate and seemed shrouded in a comfortable warm pinkish light. She spoke softly to the Naida in a strange tongue and the sparkling cluster came at her bidding to hover behind the mast. At once the huge silver-blue sail billowed out. It was emblazoned in the centre with a single silver star, fashioned after the likeness of Elrilion, the star of Elmesh.

With a slight grating noise *The Felstar* began its journey.

While Oswain handled the tiller, the Ice Maiden stood resplendent in the morning sunlight and waved goodbye to their companions on the shore.

Old Trotter raised his paw. 'May you have good success,' he repeated quietly. 'For all our sakes!'

5

The Missing Children

Oswain concentrated on piloting the unfamiliar ice-raft steadily towards the head of the River Cora, which ran from the far end of the long lake. They were moving at a fine speed, thanks to the power of the Naida and the favour of Elmesh, but it would not do to have a mishap so early in their journey.

As the yacht hissed across the ice on its wooden runners, Wheezer peered about him from his perch on the prow. They had soon left behind the greenery of the Great Forest; now the once lush landscape stretched grey and bleak as far as the eye could see. He sniffed the air. It was chill and reminded him of distant parts far to the south, when his journeyings had first taken him from warm seas to everlastingly frozen continents. Sad longings filled his heart. Why had the penguins done this, he wondered? Why was the world becoming so topsy-turvy?

His thoughts were broken by a cry of 'Here we go!' from Oswain. All at once the narrow exit was before them and the shore-line was closing in rapidly on both sides. Wheezer covered his eyes with his wings as they hurtled towards the gap. He need not have worried. In Oswain's capable hands *The Felstar* swept smoothly from the lake and on to the frozen river and soon they were skimming down its curving length towards the sea.

Not that Oswain could afford to relax. In normal times the river flowed swiftly through these upper reaches, twisting down deep gorges and through dark places where the forest overhung the banks on both sides. It took all his concentration and strength at the tiller to prevent the raft from sliding into frozen boulders or becoming entangled in the branches of overhanging trees.

''Ere, watch out! Mind the rocks,' squawked the pelican after one near miss. 'I nearly got knocked off me perch just then!'

Oswain laughed. 'You won't be the only one knocked off his perch if we hit anything at this speed, my friend. But at least you can fly. I'll just have to flap my arms and hope for the best!'

'Remind me to lend you some feathers sometime,' the bird replied. 'Hey, look out there's a tree stump sticking out of the ice straight ahead. Whoa . . . aaay . . . aay!'

Hour after hour they sped on their way in this fashion. Oswain at the tiller, Wheezer peering anxiously ahead, and the Ice Maiden silent and thoughtful with a faraway look in her eyes, and the faint bell-like music of the Naida always in the background. At length it grew dusk, but still they journeyed on, though the falling darkness made the route more treacherous than ever. Oswain's face was grim as he followed the silver thread through the fading fabric of the day.

When night had truly fallen the Ice Maiden took over the tiller. At once, an amazing transformation took place. The warm pink light surrounding her now grew in strength. Soon it engulfed the whole craft so that it glowed in the darkness and by its light the banks of the river could be dimly made out.

'Cor! Even I can see where we're going,' gasped Wheezer. He glanced up at the sail. The silver star shone in the night. It made him feel much better and he said so.

Oswain smiled. 'Yes, my friend, Loriana possesses powers from Elmesh that are given to few. We need have no fear while she steers this strange craft of ours!'

With no more sound than the hiss of its runners *The Felstar* sped through the night. But it was not unwatched. High up on the craggy banks and overhanging cliffs, dark vultures roosted in the shadows and spied the shimmering craft through hooded, knowing eyes. They were no friends of those who rode their way towards the sea.

By dawn, the little company found themselves travelling the flat wetlands which preceded the ocean, though, of course, these were now all frozen hard. Only clumps of frost-blackened reeds broke the dreary monotony of the scene.

It wasn't long before they drew near to a riverside fishing village built upon stilts and known as Corhaven. Usually a bustling little port it now looked strangely quiet and still. Oswain, who was again at the tiller, glanced up with a puzzled frown. 'I sense trouble,' he growled.

'I, too,' murmured the Ice Maiden. 'There is fear and anguish in this village, Oswain. We must interrupt our journey.'

'I agree. Though we can ill afford to do so,' he replied. 'But to ignore a cry for help is not our way. We will stop.'

With that he steered the craft to rest by a jetty alongside fishing boats frozen into the river and covered, like everything else, with white hoarfrost. It made a bleak scene in the chill grey light of a misty, wintry dawn.

Oswain and Loriana disembarked, leaving Wheezer to watch the boat. As they reached the top of the jetty steps, they were met by a heavily cloaked man who scowled at them suspiciously. In his hand he wielded a mean-looking cudgel.

'And who might you be?' he demanded. 'This is no time for strangers in our village. State your business!'

Oswain was undaunted. He looked him straight in the eye and smiled. 'We mean you no harm, my friend,' he said. 'I am Oswain, Lord of the Great Forest and son of the High King of the West. This is Loriana, the Ice Maiden, mistress of the mountains and of the Naida.'

The man lowered his cudgel and fell to one knee. Stammering with embarrassment, he said, 'I mean no harm, your Highness. I am Garvan, the headman of this village. We are loyal to the High King and good servants of Elmesh in high heaven. Our village is peace-loving, but something terrible has happened during the night and we are on the lookout for whoever or whatever has caused it.'

'What is this evil that you speak of?' the Ice Maiden asked gently. 'We sensed trouble, which is why we interrupted our journey.'

The distraught headman told them his tale of woe. Parents throughout the village had awoken that morning to find, to their horror, that all their children had mysteriously vanished. They had searched the houses and streets in vain, running to and fro calling for their loved ones, but not one was to be found. The night had simply swallowed them up without a trace.

'Then we must certainly help you find them,' Oswain declared. 'Escort us to the village square, if you will, and call all the inhabitants together.'

Ten minutes later, Oswain and Loriana were listening to the sad tale of the vanished children as sobbing mothers and anxious fathers told what they could. No one knew how the children had been awakened and captured. There were no signs of struggle, no broken windows or doors. It was as though with one accord all the children had risen from their beds and passed silently from their homes into the darkness of the night. Not a single one had been seen since.

'First this terrible ice which has prevented the coming of spring so that our food supplies are dwindling and we cannot catch fish. And now this,' groaned Garvan. 'What is going on?'

'I could tell you much about the cold,' Oswain replied. 'Though it would be of little help to you. For your encouragement, we are on our way to solve the problem – if we can. However, we will first help you solve the mystery of your lost children.'

'They cannot be far,' said Loriana. 'Let's ask Wheezer to scout the territory for us. There can be few places to hide so many children in these frozen fen lands.'

Oswain agreed and they hurried back to *The Felstar*, followed anxiously by the whole village. As soon as he was told of their plight, the old pelican set off, reminding them that his eyesight was not all that it once had been, but nonetheless promising to do what he could.

A long hour passed, during which time the villagers remained huddled together on the waterfront talking quietly among themselves, while occasionally one or other of them broke into loud sobs. Oswain and Loriana waited patiently for their companion's return.

Just as they were beginning to grow concerned for

Wheezer's safety, the Ice Maiden spotted him speeding low across the ice.

'Look!' she cried. 'Here he comes, but he is being pursued!'

Oswain whirled round just in time to see the old pelican flapping his wings for all he was worth to escape a drove of dark vultures intent on making him their prey. Nor were these ordinary carrion creatures; from their glowing eyes there flashed red beams of light which harassed him as he flew.

Wheezer didn't really stand a chance. Seconds later, the poor pelican plummeted on to the ice – not a hundred metres from where Oswain and Loriana and the villagers stood aghast. At once, with wild cries, the vultures fell upon him and their friend disappeared from their sight in a seething mass of black feathers.

'Quick!' gasped Loriana. 'Before he's killed.'

Oswain's hand flashed to his sword and it sang from its sheath. This was no ordinary blade; it was forged by Elmesh himself, and now as Oswain held it aloft in the cold grey morning light it crackled blue flame along its gleaming length. He leapt down the jetty and raced sure-footed across the ice and into the fray.

At the sound of his coming the vultures rose with harsh cries. Denied their prey, they whirled round Oswain's head, swooping angrily with snapping beaks and out-spread talons. But they were no match for the Lord of the Great Forest. His blade flashed almost too quick for the eye to see and he smote one after another of the murder-ous carrion.

Yet not one vulture fell to the ground, for each one touched by Oswain's blade simply dissolved into a puff of orange smoke. Those who watched wondered at the sight, for nothing like this had ever been seen before.

The battle did not last long. With screeches of frustrated rage the rest of the birds flew for their lives, leaving Oswain panting but victorious. He sheathed his sword and turned anxiously to where Wheezer lay still on the ice.

Loriana joined him and together they stooped to see what had become of their brave companion upon whose life hung the knowledge of where the lost children might be.

'Is he alive, or did I fight in vain?' asked Oswain. 'Pray Elmesh he is not dead.'

6

The Powers of the Ice Maiden

Loriana stretched out her hand and laid it gently on the pelican. There was no movement, no sign of life. Then she murmured words which to Oswain's listening ears seemed to speak of free skies and open seas, of salt-laden air and spice-scented islands, of endless sunlight and fish dancing in the silvery spray off far-distant shores. If he had possessed wings Oswain felt he might at this moment fly for ever.

The power of her words reached Wheezer, hovering as he was on the brink of death. He cocked open one eye, then drew in his breath with a long shuddering sigh.

'I've found the children,' he croaked.

Oswain and the Ice Maiden both smiled with relief. Wheezer was going to live. Oswain had entered the fray in the nick of time, for there are some wounds so deadly that even the Ice Maiden would not be able to undo them.

'There is hidden strength in you, old bird,' Oswain laughed. 'It was a fierce attack and you were greatly out-numbered.' His face turned serious. 'But who or what those creatures were, I do not know. Truly, they were no ordinary vultures.'

'Strange events are coming to pass in the world,' Loriana said. 'I think those creatures are the spawn of the evil that we must face and I sense that we are not done with them yet.'

Oswain nodded. 'But first we must bring back the children.' He looked down at Wheezer who was by now on his feet, ruffling his feathers and stretching his wings. 'Are you really all right, my friend?'

'Right as rain,' the bird replied, giving himself a thorough looking over. 'Reckon I'm good for a while yet. Though I began to think I was done for when those thugs attacked me. Hovering over the children they were, too.'

'Then we have come just in time,' Oswain answered grimly. 'Come on, if you are up to it, lead us to them without delay.'

Wheezer looked into the Ice Maiden's eyes. 'Thank you, ma'am,' he said.

The villagers had watched all this with amazement and, in spite of their own worries, burst into ragged cheering as the three companions reached the jetty. Oswain had a brief word with the village headman. Word that Wheezer had found the children spread like wildfire among the crowd. But no one knew yet whether they were dead or alive, and it was with considerable anxiety that the villagers watched as, led by Wheezer and under the power of the Naida, the ice yacht sped off eastwards.

Loriana standing on the prow was the first to spot something in the distance. What she saw was a glistening smooth-sided pyramid resting on the grey ice. Wheezer flew straight towards it and a few minutes later *The Felstar* drew alongside.

It was a pitiable sight. The sides of the pyramid were of clear crystal and inside were the children, from tiny toddlers to young teenagers, all hunched together in a shivering huddle. Many of the younger children were sobbing, while the older ones were doing their best to comfort them. None wore more than their night clothes and slippers and they were obviously chilled to the bone.

'What villainy is this?' growled Oswain as the raft slid to a halt beside them.

As soon as the children saw that somebody had come they crowded to the sides of the pyramid, gesturing and banging helplessly to get out. The Ice Maiden disembarked swiftly with a swirl of her gown. Walking easily on the ice she examined the strange structure from all sides. There was no sign of a door.

She began to sing as she walked. It was a haunting song, born of the high mountain ranges in springtime, when the ice cracks and streams begin to flow again, when snowdrops break through the melting snow and furry noses poke from holes as woodland creatures awake from winter slumbers. Her voice cascaded in a flood of triumphant joy, like a gush of chill water breaking over a gully and dancing down the rocks to the valley below.

Suddenly, unable to withstand the power of her song, the crystal pyramid shattered into ten thousand tiny pieces that showered harmlessly over the entombed children. They were free.

For a long moment they all stood there, wide-eyed, entranced by Loriana and her singing. Then a little girl toddled towards her with outstretched arms. The spell was broken and in an instant the Ice Maiden was surrounded by a bustle of children all wanting to reach out and touch her.

Oswain stood on the prow of the boat with his hands on his hips and laughed out loud at the happy sight. 'Good morning, children,' he called. 'We've come to take you all home. Welcome aboard *The Felstar*.'

A feeble cheer rose from the freezing children. Then, assisted by Oswain and Loriana, they began to clamber aboard the craft. There were about fifty in all and they clung to every part of the boat. Loriana spoke to the Naida and *The Felstar* swung round at her bidding, with its huge silver-blue sail billowing forth. Soon they were speeding back to the village.

Many of the children were suffering badly from the cruel effects of the cold and simply couldn't stop shivering. 'Time for some medicine, I think,' the Ice Maiden observed and from her gown drew out a silver flask. Each child was given a small sip of the cordial. The effect was startling. Colour returned to their cheeks and before long they were chattering nineteen to the dozen and climbing all over the craft, as though their ordeal had been no more than a day's outing.

'I'm not sure that was such a good idea!' croaked Wheezer, as two of the children nearly knocked him off his perch.

Soon they were drawing near to the village, watched by the crowd of anxious parents on the dockside. A great cheer arose when they realised that all the children were safe and sound. Minutes later the air was filled with the buzz and chatter of joyful families being reunited.

'We must find out what happened in the night,' said Oswain once the children were safe and sound in their parents' care. He spoke with the headman and ten minutes later a boy and a girl were ushered into their presence. The boy's name was Filban and the girl's Gisana.

Filban was the first to speak in answer to their questions. 'I thought I was dreaming,' he said. 'Something seemed to wake me. A bright orange light it was, and music. It sort of filled the room.'

'What was the music like?' the Ice Maiden enquired.

'I dunno,' he said. 'Never heard anything like it before. It was sort of rhythmic but it sounded like a harp or something like that, but I couldn't tell you what the tune was.'

'And the light danced to the music,' Gisana interrupted. 'It flickered very, very fast. At first it made my head ache, but I got used to it, and then I just wanted to get up and follow it. I don't know why,' she ended lamely.

'But didn't you feel the cold?' Oswain asked.

'No, I don't think so. At least I don't remember that,' Filban replied. 'We just followed the light and the sound of the music. I don't know how long for.'

'And this is what all the children are saying?' Garvan asked.

The two children nodded.

'Then what?'

'Then the light vanished and the music stopped and we were in the dark and it was very cold,' said Filban.

'We didn't know where we were,' said Gisana. 'It was terribly dark and freezing. We knew we were out on the ice somewhere but when we tried to walk we found we were trapped by invisible walls.' She shuddered. 'I thought we were all going to die.'

'And when day came we saw that the walls of our prison were made of glass, or ice. But I don't think it was either, really,' Filban continued. 'We tried to break them but they were too strong. Then we saw vultures flying overhead and we were glad to be inside.' He smiled ruefully. 'Well, you know what I mean.'

Oswain nodded.

'There was nothing else to see, so we just stood there in the cold, waiting. We're so glad you came,' Gisana added.

Oswain smiled and thanked the children. When they had gone he turned to Loriana. 'This is a bad business and no mistake.'

The Ice Maiden pondered the matter. 'Was it just some spiteful act done for no reason, or was it meant to slow us down? Or were the children perhaps needed for some evil purpose? Surely that is it!' she cried. 'They were being watched over by those vultures because something or someone wanted them alive.'

'Whoever they are, they must be heartless brutes to kidnap children like that. What did they want with them?' Oswain wondered. 'And how many other children have experienced a similar fate? I'm certain it's all connected to our quest.' He paused. 'Filban and Gisana said the light was orange. Didn't Wheezer and Horatio also say something about an orange light over the penguins who stole the South Pole? I think I'm beginning to understand what is going on. Loriana, we must travel as fast as we can to Aethius!'

There was nothing more to be done in the village of Corhaven and so, after receiving the heartfelt thanks of the people who lived there, the company once more set sail towards the mysterious island where they hoped to find the answers to their questions.

The land was soon left far behind and they were now skimming across the frozen sea. Slowly the bleakness of the dawn gave way to brighter skies, and from the light of the sun they could now set their course for the island of Aethius and whatever awaited them there.

For two days and nights they sailed uneventfully across

the frozen wastes, Oswain and Loriana taking turns at the tiller while Wheezer kept a sharp lookout for any sign of the vultures; but he saw none. Only the occasional lonely seabird crossed their path, intent on some business of its own.

By early morning on the third day Oswain judged that they must be nearing the island, and sure enough, as the sun rose they could just make out a smudge on the horizon which indicated land, though doubtless it would be as frozen as the sea.

The smudge grew larger and to their dismay they found they were speeding into a long rolling bank of fog. Within minutes the sun had dimmed to a ghost and a pale mist folded around *The Felstar* like a cold wet blanket.

'We shall have to be careful that we don't just run head-long into the island,' Oswain warned.

'I sense something more,' the Ice Maiden replied. There was an uneasy edge to her voice. 'Danger lies before us, though in what form I cannot tell.'

Even as she spoke, Wheezer called from the prow. 'Look out! There's something ahead!'

Alerted by his warning they stared intently through the dim light. The only sound to be heard was the hiss of their craft. All around, the grey mist pressed in upon them, but straight ahead it was different. An orange light glowed fuzzily through the fog. It was sickly, eerie and unnatural – and they were speeding straight towards its centre!

7

Inside Tergan's Lair

If Peter and Andrew had expected the wild boy to wait for them outside their cubicle, they were mistaken. He was off like a shot and it was all they could do to keep up with him as he twisted and turned through the icy corridors. On several occasions one or other of them narrowly avoided slipping over on the treacherous surface.

Peter was in the lead as they hared round a particularly tight bend. To his dismay, he lost his footing completely and went down on the ice with a hard bump. Andrew was so close behind that he ran straight into him and went sprawling as well.

'Ouch!' he cried. 'That hurt!'

'Sorry,' panted his brother as they scrambled to their feet and regained their bearings. Ahead of them the tunnel branched three ways, but the wild boy was nowhere to be seen.

'Oh, no! We've lost him. Which way has he gone?' groaned Peter.

Fortunately, their dismay didn't last long. They heard a 'psst' by their feet and saw the wild boy's tousled head grinning up at them from a small tunnel leading off to the left. It was no more than knee high and they might never have noticed it if Peter hadn't fallen over when he did.

'S'ppose we'll have to follow him?' Andrew said doubt-fully as the boy's head ducked back into the gloom.

'We've got no choice really, have we?' Peter agreed.

So, with an anxious glance both ways to see that the coast was clear, they crawled into the tunnel, Andrew fol-lowing Peter. It was pitch dark inside and all they could hear were the sounds of their breathing and of the wild boy scrambling ahead of them. Peter pressed on and tried to catch him up – not that he had much chance, the boy moved far too quickly for that!

They had no idea of the time or of how long they had crawled like this, but after a while they began to notice an uncomfortable change. The ice was melting and soon their hands and knees were sloshing through cold, wet slush.

The further they continued, the warmer it became, and the furs for which they had been so grateful now made them feel far too hot. Both boys were soon perspiring heavily. With sweat running down their faces and sting-ing their eyes in the darkness, and their trousers soaked through with freezing cold water, they began to wish they had never started following the wild boy. And all the while there was the nagging worry about what had become of their sister.

Gradually the ground grew dry and before long they were crawling on hard rock. Then Peter realised that he could see a little bit. Not much to be sure, but he could make out the dim shadow of the boy in front of him. The rocky walls of the passage were lit with a dull reddish hue.

'Must be coming to the end of this,' he called back to Andrew. 'At least, I can see some kind of light. Dunno why it's getting warmer, though. I thought this whole place was frozen.'

'I don't even care,' Andrew responded. 'I just want to get out of this rotten tunnel!'

The tunnel climbed for a while and then, as Peter had guessed, it came to a sudden end. The wild boy scrambled through the exit and disappeared.

Like an overgrown mouse, Peter poked his head out of the hole and took a cautious look around. They were entering a large cavern whose walls glowed bright red. He blinked and squinted in the light, then looked up in amazement at the soaring dome. It must have been at least a hundred metres high, and so long that he could barely make out the far end. The vaulted walls flickered and glistened like coals in a fire. The air was hot and smelt of sulphur. Glad of the chance to get off his hands and knees, he scrambled through the tunnel mouth and stood up.

The next moment he wished he hadn't. For Peter found he was standing on a narrow ledge above a chasm which was all of three hundred metres deep. And down below he could see the source of the light and the heat. White-hot lava flowed and frothed from the rocks in great rivulets and puddles. The hot air hit him with searing force and he drew back with a cry of alarm.

'What is it, Peter?' called Andrew as he scrambled out to join his brother. 'Whooa! What's that? Where on earth are we?' he gasped when he saw the fiery chasm.

'Somewhere inside a live volcano I should think,' Peter replied. 'Whew, it's so hot! And doesn't it stink!'

None of this seemed to bother the wild boy. He was

grinning from ear to ear as he beckoned them to follow him.

This wasn't easy, for the path was only about a metre wide and snaked in a dark ribbon across the almost sheer cliff face. Very cautiously, the boys followed their guide, keeping as far from the edge as they could.

'Try not to look down,' Peter gasped to his brother as they edged along with their backs to the rugged wall. Both boys were coughing constantly by now and their eyes stung with the heat and the smell of sulphur.

In one place the path had vanished altogether, and they had to step across a narrow gap with nothing below them except the subterranean fire. It took all the courage they had and they could feel the searing heat of the lava welling up like the blast from a furnace. One slip would have meant certain death.

After what seemed an age, they came at last to a wide platform of rock. Much to their relief, it stretched back into a broad tunnel which ran off into the dark. Anything seemed better than staying in this cavern.

The wild boy stood almost on the edge of the rocky platform and beckoned to them. Peter and Andrew hesitated. They felt they had had enough of precipices for one night and were reluctant to join him. However, at his insistence, they went across. He was pointing down into the fiery pit.

'Tergan. Tergan's lair,' he said.

At first, neither could see what he was indicating. All they could make out were the rivers of lava. Then Andrew saw what he was getting at.

'Pete!' he gasped. 'Can you see what I can see? Look, it's a great fire-eating monster.'

'It's a dragon,' said Peter grimly.

They stared in amazement. There, half sunk in the boiling, fuming lava, yet quite unharmed, lay sleeping the most enormous dragon imaginable. It was a vast, heaving, glowing red hulk with a body at least two hundred metres long, they guessed, and that was without taking into account its coiled neck. Or rather necks. For the dragon had many heads, and its serpentine necks were coiled around one another like a pile of gigantic, glistening, red snakes.

'Tergan, he sleep,' exclaimed the wild boy. 'Now we sleep, too. We safe from Stribs.'

'Sleep? Here? You've got to be joking!' coughed Peter incredulously. He had no idea whether the boy understood him or not.

'What happens if that dragon wakes up, or . . . or if the volcano erupts?' demanded Andrew as they backed away from the cliff edge.

The wild boy didn't reply but led them over to the mouth of the tunnel where a cooler breeze blew and where the air was fresh. He pointed to the ground and, without saying another word, lay down and instantly fell fast asleep, leaving the two boys standing there like dummies.

Andrew looked at Peter and shrugged his shoulders. 'Now what? Do we stay here?'

'I suppose so,' Peter replied. 'But I'm worried about Sarah. What will she do when she finds we're gone? Supposing they kill her or something? I thought he was going to help us rescue her. At least, I hoped he was.'

'Well, maybe he will in the morning, but there's nothing we can do at the moment, is there? Look at him. He's fast asleep!' Andrew replied. 'Come on, Pete, we'd better get some rest. I'm completely knackered.'

* * *

Sarah, meanwhile, was almost asleep on her feet. She was sick and tired of crystals and coloured liquids. In fact, by now she didn't know which was which and they were no more than a blur before her eyes. As for that stupid wire pyramid. . . .

Yet, still the penguins made her work. They wouldn't even let her have a drink and her thirst was becoming unbearable, worse even than the hunger which she had felt earlier. Raaz himself was busily writing down everything she did while the watchful Stribs stood around her with their spears at the ready. There was no way she could escape.

Weary hours dragged by. Every time one of her mixtures was placed under the wire pyramid it was the same. Nothing. Not even a little spark. Against her better judgement she cried tears of frustration.

Faint at first but growing stronger as she grew weaker, was an insistent voice, a woman's voice, telling her to call for help. Something told her it wasn't a good voice and she refused to listen.

At last, she had had enough. 'I'm sick and tired of all this!' she cried. With one last burst of energy she swept the crystals and liquids off the table and sent them crashing to the floor where they splintered and splashed in all directions. Then, no longer minding what happened to her, she flopped down and began to sob her heart out.

The Strat was furious and several times struck her hard with his flipper. But, though it hurt and made her cry louder, Sarah was past caring. All she wanted to do was sleep.

At the Strat's command the Stribs dragged her to her feet and led her from the chamber. She stumbled as she went, but a flood of relief filled her as she anticipated at last getting some rest, and something to drink.

However, it was not to be. Instead of returning her to the sleeping quarters, they took her back to the main dome where she was dragged before Yarx. Sarah looked up at him from haggard and tearstained eyes. She could barely focus and her head felt dizzy.

The chief Strat approached her until his beak was only a flipper's width from her face. He cocked his head to one side and his right eye seemed to burn like a bright point of light which bored into hers. Sarah tried to turn her head away but found it was impossible. Her brain was filled with two fuzzy circles of red and yellow light, and music, the music of something like a harp. She knew she was losing control of her mind but no longer had the energy to do anything about it.

Dimly, in the far distance, she saw Oswain and Loriana and the greenery of the Great Forest, but the picture in her mind grew dimmer and soon faded. The two sets of throbbing, pulsating circles became one until there was nothing else except red and yellow light. She felt something touch her cracked lips, and tasted a cool, slightly bitter liquid. She took a sip, cautiously at first, then another, and another. Thirst overtook her and she gulped at the liquid eagerly.

Then slowly the hypnotic light and the music began to fade and she could see again. Sarah no longer felt weary and she stood upright of her own accord, facing the Strat without fear.

'Who are you and what is your purpose?' he asked.

Sarah looked him directly in the eye.

'I am Strib 616 and I am here to serve you, Lord Yarx!' she answered.

8

The Voice in the Mist

'*Amar lei, Naida!*' cried the Ice Maiden.

At her powerful command, the billowing sail drooped around the mast and the ice yacht began to slow. But it didn't stop. In spite of Oswain's efforts at the tiller, an unseen force continued to draw the craft deeper into the mist and on towards the ominous orange light.

Silently the three companions waited to see what would befall them. Soon *The Felstar* was bathed in a sickly orange glow and everything, themselves included, glistened unnaturally pale, as though all true colours had been washed out of the world. The air seemed thundery and a heaviness pressed in on them from all sides.

Then a voice began to thrum. Deep, menacing, rhythmical, it filled the air and assailed their minds. 'Bow down and serve! Bow down and serve! Bow down and serve!'

Wheezer cowered into a corner with his wings over his head, trying to resist the awful sound. Fear possessed him and he was trembling all over.

Neither Oswain nor Loriana would be cowed by this loathsome voice. They had long ago learned to respect strong foes, but not to be afraid of them. 'We serve only Elmesh,' Oswain cried out loud. 'We bow to no one else!'

At this their craft was thrown violently out of control and began to twist and weave across the ice at such speed that it was in danger of capsizing. Clutching the creaking

71

timbers as best they could, the companions saw that they were racing towards a cluster of crystal pyramids, identical to the one from which they had rescued the children of Corhaven. Unless they did something quickly they were going to crash straight into them.

'Enough of this!' Oswain called to Loriana. He clambered to his feet and, balancing precariously on the bucking deck, unsheathed his sword. The blade burned with bright blue fire as he raised it aloft. At that same instant the Ice Maiden issued a strong command to the Naida. The air filled once more with their high bell-like tinkle and the sail billowed out as though a strong clean wind had cut right through the stagnant mist which surrounded them.

At once The Felstar came under control. With Loriana standing behind the sail, her arms raised in support of the Naida, and Oswain holding his burning sword aloft, The Felstar began to speed forward again on a straight course. Together, they began to sing.

> 'Laris semperi cora teran
> So pora Elma nah lepo
> Simpiri vecta tromara pelan
> Nai loma tora si chorei
> Omparesta ni sera lei
> To semarenda etresa
> Elmi kera lo semareso
> Li tritera lei Elma!'

Their harmony was rich, confident and exultant, and Wheezer felt courage flow back into his cowering frame. There was no need to fear the voice from the mist when he had friends like these! He stood up on his perch, spread his wings and began to caw defiantly at whatever the foul force was that opposed them.

My voice isn't very tuneful, he thought. *But I'll sing with the best of them!*

* * *

Sarah had been busy, meanwhile. From the time that she had come under the power of Yarx all the tiredness had left her. She had returned willingly to her work bench and begun again mixing the crystals and the coloured liquids which they set before her. With renewed strength, she worked diligently through the night, and when dawn broke outside, like a true Strib, she readily ate the raw fish which they offered her and she joined in with their chant.

She seemed to have developed some skill at this strange chemistry and each time her experiments were placed under the pyramid a few sparks flashed through the orange glow. The Strat was very pleased with the results and eagerly pored over the notes which he had written.

Then it happened. She succeeded at last. As the pyramid began to turn at Raaz's chant, flashes of fire danced over the crystals so that they now began to glow with an inner fire of their own. The liquids hissed and bubbled. Faster and faster the pyramid span until it was no more than a blur of light, and a high pitched zinging sound filled the air.

At length it began to slow down and when it came to rest, there, suspended in space in the centre of the pyramid, hung a single, large crystal filled with orange light. Sarah gazed at it blankly.

Raaz was delighted.

'We have done it!' he breathed. 'We have created the Key.' He turned to the surrounding Stribs. 'Call Lord Yarx and Senator Kig at once. This is a Strat order which must be obeyed!'

* * *

Sarah's success came just as Oswain, Loriana and Wheezer were speeding away from the orange light and into the ordinary grey mist.

At that very moment, as the crystal was being formed, there was a dazzling flash behind them. It was accompanied by a deafening roar, and before they could do anything about it The Felstar was struck by a huge thunderbolt which threw all three on to the deck where they lay stunned by the force of the blow. Almost at once, the craft burst into flames and began to burn furiously.

As if that was not enough, before they could regain their wits, The Felstar gave a violent lurch. With a loud crunching and cracking the ice broke beneath its runners. Their once sleek ice yacht was now no more than a lumbering wreck heaving on the ocean swell. The only question was what it would do first – capsize into the sea or burn out. Either way, the situation did not look very hopeful for the three companions.

Meanwhile, Peter and Andrew had been fast asleep in the underground cavern. Sheer exhaustion had overcome their fear of the dragon and they had not stirred all night. But now they were awakened by a loud hissing sound.

Peter leapt up. 'What's that?' he gasped.

The wild boy was already awake and urging Andrew to his feet 'Tergan! Tergan stirs!' he cried.

The hissing grew louder. Then to Peter's horror one of the dragon's huge heads rose from the pit below. Its scaly skin glowed blood red and its baleful eyes burned bright as it twisted and turned this way and that. White hot lava ran dripping and splashing from its horns and even from its sabre-toothed jaws. The air was filled with the stench of burning sulphur and the sound of crackling fire.

'Run for it!' Peter shouted.

Nobody needed any persuading. All three turned and bolted for the tunnel as fast as their legs could carry them.

The tunnel proved to be quite short and, suddenly, to Peter and Andrew's immense relief, they emerged into bright daylight. They were none too soon. Moments after the boys were clear of the entrance a huge tongue of yellow flame billowed out after them.

'Wow!' gasped Andrew as he staggered backwards. 'Thank goodness we got out when we did.'

'You're telling me!' Peter panted.

The two brothers took stock of where they were. To their surprise they were no longer looking upon frozen wasteland but on lush green vegetation and a riot of flowers. Below them stretched a jungle valley steaming in the hot morning sun, and they could hear birds chirruping in the trees.

Beyond the jungle lay the sea, calm and blue – though not far from the shore everything was shrouded in a bank of mist. Clearly, nothing was frozen on this part of the coast.

'What kind of weird place is this?' Andrew wondered.

'Dunno, but it's a flipping sight better than where we were,' said Peter. 'Hey, where's wild boy gone? We still don't even know his name.'

In answer to his question, the boy suddenly came bounding out of the bushes. His arms were laden with all kinds of colourful fruit and berries.

'Eat,' he offered.

After nearly a day and a half without any meals they needed little encouragement. Soon they were savouring their first breakfast since their adventure had begun.

'I'm starving!' mumbled Andrew through a mouthful of breadfruit.

'Me too,' his brother agreed.

Just as he said this, Peter happened to glance up at the sea. He frowned. Something appeared to be glowing at the edge of the mist. He stopped eating and stared at it open-mouthed.

'What's up, Pete?' Andrew asked as he bit into a juicy apple.

His brother pointed out to sea. Emerging from the mist was some kind of boat, but it was listing badly in the water and its timbers and sail were all ablaze. All three rose to their feet and watched anxiously as the stricken craft drifted helplessly towards the shore.

'We'd better get down there and see if we can help,' Peter decided. He turned to the wild boy and pointed at the flaming boat. 'Sea. To the sea,' he said. 'We go. Show us the way.'

The wild boy nodded enthusiastically and at once began to run down the hill.

'Quick, follow him or we'll lose him again,' said Peter,

and together they plunged into the jungle in pursuit of their elusive guide.

By the time they reached the pebbly shoreline the strange and ungainly boat was almost there too. It was barely afloat and still burning.

'There are two people on board,' gasped Peter as he laboured along the beach. 'Look!'

Even as he spoke, the craft ground on to the shallows and they saw a man and a woman clambering over the side and into the water. A large and ungainly sea bird fluttered ahead of them, seemingly surrounded by a twinkling aura of light.

Peter and Andrew reached them just as they were wading on to the beach. Neither could believe their eyes.

'It's Oswain!' gasped Andrew.

'And Loriana!' exclaimed Peter.

Oswain and the Ice Maiden's faces broke into smiles of joy upon seeing their old friends so unexpectedly.

'Peter and Andrew,' cried Oswain. 'Elmesh be praised! Well met, indeed! But what a way to find us, like a couple of drowned rats!' He threw his strong arms around them both and lifted them off their feet.

The Ice Maiden bent and kissed them. 'This is a wondrous matter to be sure,' she said. 'Even though his star burns bright and clear for all to see, the ways of Elmesh are mysterious, indeed!' She shook the water from her hair. 'You must tell us how you come to be here. And where is Sarah?'

Peter began to explain how they had landed themselves once again in Oswain and Loriana's world, though whereabouts he hadn't a clue. 'And then we saw this wild boy and followed him, and that's when we got caught by . . . by, would you believe, penguins.' He turned to introduce their rescuer. But the boy was nowhere to be seen.

'Now where's he gone?' Andrew groaned, scanning the beach in vain.

'He'll probably turn up again soon,' Peter said hopefully. 'I expect he was shy, or afraid of you. We don't even know who he is yet.'

'Well, we can at least introduce our companion,' said Oswain. Whereupon he presented them to the courageous Wheezer, who said he was delighted to meet those of whom by now he had heard so many deeds of renown.

Sitting together in the morning sun, watching the remains of *The Felstar* burn out while the Naida hovered nearby, they quickly shared their different experiences.

'It is a grim tale of sinister forces,' said Oswain at length. 'But one thing is quite clear. We must first rescue Sarah from the clutches of those penguins.'

'I have never known such creatures to be bad,' said the Ice Maiden. 'The evil that has possessed them is truly great, and it all points in one direction.'

They were interrupted by a rumble out to sea. Everyone looked to see what was happening.

At first there was nothing obvious. Then it dawned on them. The bank of mist was on the move. Oswain observed it grimly. It was drifting rapidly towards them.

'Oh boy!' groaned Peter as the sun was blotted out. 'Now what's going to happen?'

9

In Search of Sarah

Oswain and Loriana stood to their feet, together with Peter and Andrew. They watched silently as the ominous bank of mist curled towards them. Wheezer took to the air, hoping to fly above it. His wings flapped loudly, breaking the eerie stillness that had fallen. Even the sound of the sea was dulled and it lapped feebly against the shore as though the power in the mist had drained away all its strength. There was little the companions could do but wait, and hope. Oswain drew in his breath sharply as the first stray fingers of mist brushed the beach.

Then, as though driven by some artful intelligence, the mist quite suddenly veered off to their right and began to pour up the side of the island. Inside five minutes it had settled as a ball of cloud crowning the volcano, and only the faint orange glow in its centre betrayed the fact that anything was wrong.

'Whew, that's a relief!' gasped Andrew. 'I didn't fancy trying to fight fog!'

'It was warning us off,' said Oswain. 'Whatever is in there thinks that we are an irritation but not yet a danger.'

'Hm, but it's still not going to help us rescue Sarah, is it?' Peter replied. 'We can't get to her from the top now and I don't fancy trying to take on that dragon. What did that boy call it – Tergan?'

'Yeah,' said Andrew, glancing around. 'Huh, where has that boy got to?'

'There he is, just behind those bushes,' yelled Peter as he caught a glimpse of the boy's face.

'Well, don't chase him or you'll frighten him away again. Hoi, wild boy,' Andrew called, 'it's all right. These are friends of ours. They'll help us.'

'Come and talk,' Peter added.

Very cautiously, the boy crept from behind the bushes and approached them. He looked ready to run away at any moment. Oswain took a step forward and held up his hand in peace.

'I am Oswain,' he said as the boy came within range. 'And this is Loriana. We wish to be friends. What is your name?'

'Oswain?' the boy repeated. 'You Oswain, friend?' Suddenly, his wariness disappeared and he broke into a big smile. 'Me, Rag. I friend and I help you. And you, Lo-Loriana, I help too, 'cos you pretty lady!'

Peter and Andrew grinned and for the first time they were all able to introduce themselves properly. Wheezer fluttered down to join them and soon, much to Andrew's delight, they were sharing another breakfast together on the sea shore.

'Time for a council of war,' Oswain declared. 'We find ourselves met on the island of Aethius, and somewhere inside the volcano the penguins have hidden the South Pole. Clearly they are up to something terrible but we don't yet know what that is.'

'But they've got Sarah,' interjected Andrew as he helped himself to more dates.

'Yes,' said the Ice Maiden. 'And we must rescue her from the clutches of those penguins as soon as we can.'

'Then there is this strange cloud we went through – and there's some power at work in that!' Oswain continued.

'Do you have any idea what this is all about?' Peter asked. 'I mean, kids trapped in frozen pyramids, weird vultures, crazy penguins – and then we find a dragon half asleep in a live volcano. I just can't hack it.'

Oswain gave him a taut-lipped smile. 'We aren't sure yet but from what you've told us and from our own experiences it all points in one direction.' He glanced at the Ice Maiden. 'It's possible that an evil being that we do not even care to name in Elmar or Alamore is trying to break into Caris Meriac for a second time, and maybe . . . maybe is being aided by someone else whom we have encountered in the past.'

'It certainly looks that way,' Loriana agreed.

'Who are these people, and what do you mean "break in"?' Andrew asked.

Oswain leaned forward and clasped his hands together in front of him. 'It's too long a story to tell now, but years ago before I was born, my father, King Argil, whom you probably think is a bit past it, was a mighty and courageous warrior. He is not the High King for nothing. He fought a foe so terrible that if he had not won, the whole of Caris Meriac would have sunk into unbelievable evil. You see, his fight was against a being – some call him a demon, some a god – that entered our world from another realm.'

'You mean like us?' said Peter.

'Yes, but very different. There are many realms and many doors but not all of them are safe,' Oswain explained. 'In one of these realms the people, led by an arrogant and power-crazed man, began to build a great and dark fortress that stretched up to heaven. He and all his gathered forces determined to wage war on Elmesh, though he is known by other names there. They opened doors between worlds by force and without wisdom and began great wars that shook the heavens.'

'Did they win?' Andrew asked.

'Oh, yes, they won, or at least they thought they had, but all they had done was to destroy the idea of Elmesh in some people's heads.'

'Elmesh is the Creator of all the universes and he is the source of all love and truth,' said the Ice Maiden. 'He cannot be unmade.'

'That's what I thought,' said Peter.

'Still, in their folly they brought great suffering upon many and they opened doors to evil that were best kept closed,' Oswain said.

'And that's what let this . . . this thing in?' ventured Andrew.

Oswain nodded. 'And more besides as we were to find out later, even after this particular evil was banished.'

'Are you allowed to tell us his name? I mean, why don't you speak about him? Is it banned, or something?' Andrew asked.

Oswain shook his head. 'No, there is no ban. It is just that he is so disgustingly bad that we prefer not to mention him. But I will tell you, for I suspect that this is what we are up against. His name – and he has others in other worlds – his name is Shugob the Devourer.'

There was silence for a moment and a chill gust blew from the mountain. Peter gave a shiver. 'I'm not sure if I want to know this,' he said. 'But what does he do that makes him so rotten?'

Oswain's face hardened with anger. 'He feeds on children,' he said. 'Always he feeds on children. In some worlds they had to burn their children alive to satisfy him; in others they had to kill them before they were born, and in Caris Meriac . . .'

Peter had heard enough. He rose to his feet and his face was tight. 'We've got to rescue my sister,' he said. 'And we've got to do it now.'

Nobody wanted to disagree and as they all stood, the wild boy, Rag, who had been listening intently, trying to understand all that they were saying, became very excited.

'Children, I show you children. Many children like me,' he exclaimed.

The others turned to him in amazement.

'You mean there are other children on this island?' Oswain demanded.

Rag nodded energetically.

'But we thought you were the only one,' said Andrew. 'Like a . . . like a boy Friday,' he ended lamely as he saw the puzzled looks on everyone's faces, except Peter's.

'Can you take us to them?' Loriana asked gently.

'Me take you. But it dangerous. They all prisoners. I escape. Rag always escape,' he answered proudly.

'But first Sarah,' said Oswain firmly as he rose to his feet. 'Do you know a way to the penguins' camp which doesn't go near the dragon?' he asked Rag.

The boy frowned. 'Very hard,' he replied. 'I know hard way.'

'Hard or not, we must take it,' the Ice Maiden replied. 'I feel Sarah is in grave danger.'

So Rag led the party back into the jungle and steadily

up the side of the mountain until the forest began to thin. They came out quite abruptly on to bare rock, only to find that their path was blocked by a yawning chasm which fell away to the steaming depths of the jungle far below. All were surprised to see how far they had climbed.

'Have we come the wrong way?' Andrew asked hopefully as he saw what lay before them. But Rag was pointing to a small cave on the far cliff face, for the chasm was actually a deep V cut back into the mountainside. 'We go there,' he said.

'How on earth do we reach that?' groaned Peter in dismay.

But already Rag was edging his way along a narrow ledge that led into the point of the gully where the two cliff faces met. Though this traverse seemed just as bad as the path inside Tergan's lair, the others had no choice but to follow their fearless and nimble guide and to hope for the best.

'It's all right for you!' Andrew called to Wheezer, as he edged round a tricky lump of rock. The pelican was hovering right next to him, riding the warm upcurrents from the forest below. 'You don't have to worry about falling.'

In spite of their fears the party made surprisingly good progress across the rock face and were soon working back along the opposite face of the V towards the mouth of the cave.

They had almost reached the cave when disaster struck. Andrew lost his footing. With a cry of dismay he slipped from the path and before he could do anything to stop himself, tumbled helplessly into the gorge. The others froze with horror.

Andrew could feel himself falling backwards in slow

motion. He could see his friends on the ledge diminishing in size as he dropped. He thought his whole life should be rushing by him, as in the movies. But it wasn't. He was just falling.

Before he could muster another thought, he hit something so hard that it knocked the breath right out of him. Mercifully, it wasn't the ground but a bush growing out of the cliff. Gasping with pain he scrabbled and grabbed at the branches, tearing desperately at the leaves to get a grip before it was too late. Somehow he managed, and he clung breathless and shaking to the bouncing branches, for a moment unable to believe his good fortune.

Wheezer flew down and hovered alongside him.

'Wheezer,' he gasped. 'Help me!'

Without hesitation, the old pelican dropped away into the jungle below. It seemed an age before he returned and Andrew feared that the tree might give way at any moment. All his companions could do was to shout encouragement from up above.

At long last Wheezer flew into sight. In his beak he carried several lengths of creeper. Oswain, standing high above, took the vines from Wheezer and swiftly knotted them together. Then he threw one end down to Andrew.

'Well done, Wheezer,' he said loudly. But to the others he muttered, 'This isn't going to be easy. We must get to the cave and try to make this creeper fast or we'll all be pulled off with him.'

Reaching the cave, they managed to wedge the creeper between some cracked rock at the entrance.

Oswain called down to Andrew. 'Tie the end around your waist, Andrew. Use a good knot.'

Andrew had learned how to tie a bowline and he began

to secure the creeper to his waist. Not that it was easy, lying precariously on a bush halfway down a cliff and needing both hands to tie the knot. But he succeeded at last and gave his rescuers the go-ahead.

'You'll have to let yourself go,' cried Oswain, as he and the others took the strain.

'And pray Elmesh the line holds,' added Loriana.

Letting go was the hardest moment in Andrew's life. He looked down at the forest below and the broken jagged rocks at the foot of the cliff. The airy spaciousness made him feel light-headed and a bit sick.

The tree trembled beneath him and everything within him said to hold on tighter. Fear rose up in his throat and he wanted to cry. He just wished there was some other way of getting off the fragile perch. Desperately, he looked around to see if it were possible to climb down the cliff. But there was no other choice.

He looked up at the sheer cliff above. There, to his right, was Oswain's encouraging face and trailing upwards the slender vine on which his life depended. He began to take deep breaths. Then, gripping the creeper so tightly that his knuckles were white, Andrew launched himself from the tree.

He swung like a pendulum along the face of the cliff and hit the rock with a hard thump, spinning and bouncing and grazing his knuckles. The creeper stretched and creaked under his weight and for one heart-stopping moment he thought it would break.

The line held, and seconds later he could feel himself being pulled up by the willing hands above. He tried to scrabble at the rock with his feet to help. The haul seemed to take an age and he could hear his companions puffing and panting above. At last, he could make out Oswain's hands heaving away. He was almost at the top.

Then, suddenly, there was a ripping, creaking sound and to his horror he felt the creeper beginning to tear. 'Quick!' he gasped as he managed to get one hand on to the rocky ledge. The vine gave way and for an instant he seemed to hang in space. In a flash, Oswain dropped to his knees and seized Andrew's hand just as it was slipping off the edge.

Time froze; then, slowly and painfully, Andrew felt Oswain pull him up over the ledge to the safety of the cave. He heard Peter give a faint cheer as he flopped on to the rock. Then he passed out.

Everyone felt drained by the events. For a moment they all sat puffing and blowing, unable to speak a word.

'Elmesh be praised,' Oswain breathed at length. 'That was a near thing.'

The Ice Maiden stroked Andrew's head. He was still white and shaking. He had come round quickly but when he tried to stand up, his legs just collapsed under him. She drew her flask and gave him a drink. 'This should help,' she said.

The Ice Maiden's cordial had remarkable power and the effect on Andrew was almost instantaneous. The colour flooded back into his cheeks and almost before you knew it he was his old self again.

'The wings aren't quite right yet,' he grinned. 'Oh well, back to the drawing board!' His brother took a relieved swipe at him.

'We go,' said Rag.

The tunnel proved to be safe and though their path twisted and turned for what seemed miles they passed through its length uneventfully – something for which Andrew was very thankful.

Rag knew where he was going without the aid of any light, but the others were grateful for the crystal ring which the Ice Maiden wore. She held the ring aloft and a sapphire light bathed their path.

The air grew cooler the further they went and the tunnel, which had been dry underfoot at the start, was now slushy. Soon they were walking on solid ice. 'We must be getting near the penguins' camp,' Peter whispered. Rag put his finger to his lips and slowed the pace to a crawl.

They came out on what Peter realised was the shelf of ice where they had spotted Rag on the first morning of their captivity. Before them stretched the large ice cavern. To their relief it appeared empty and Peter remembered that all the Stribs would be busy at their tasks for the day.

The ledge wasn't high and it was possible to descend to the floor quite easily by means of a path to the right. The Ice Maiden, who feared no frozen thing, skipped lithely down.

Just at that very moment, alone and unaccompanied, Sarah herself entered the cavern from the far end. Loriana spotted her at once.

'Sarah,' she called. 'Sarah, over here. It's me, Loriana.'

The girl stopped dead and looked in the direction of the voice. She seemed rooted to the spot. The Ice Maiden hastened joyfully towards her, but slowed down thoughtfully and wonderingly, as she drew near. All of a sudden, Sarah's face contorted into a frightful grimace. She raised her hands in claw-like menace and spat.

'Bow down and worship!' she cried. 'Bow down and

worship. This is a Strib order which must be obeyed. Worship Shugob the Almighty!'

The force of her words stopped the Ice Maiden. To those watching, the faint pink aura which always surrounded her grew in strength, as though she were facing an unseen darkness.

'Come with me, Sarah,' she said. Loriana spoke softly but command was in her voice.

'I am Strib 616. Bow down and worship Shugob the Almighty!' Sarah cried in response. The air around her glowed orange and the watchers felt the chill of bleak, empty darkness as it did so. She seemed possessed of a terrible power.

Grimacing, and with a threatening snarl, she began to wave her arms at the Ice Maiden. The orange aura grew in intensity and Sarah's arms looked like two whirling, slashing scythes. Loriana began to shimmer brighter and brighter. To those watching it seemed that two great powers were locked in struggle, light against light – and they appeared to be equally matched. Then with a fierce cry Sarah slashed the air with her arm. To the horror of those watching, the fiery blade of light sliced into the Ice Maiden and her form shattered into a thousand glittering fragments – then promptly disappeared.

Oswain leaped forward and his hand flashed to his sword. But there was absolutely nothing he could do. Not a trace of the Ice Maiden was anywhere to be seen.

10

The Lyre Player

Mrs Trotter and Stiggle had made good progress. They had set out westwards from the Great Forest shortly before Trotter and the forest-folk had journeyed south to build the ice yacht for Oswain and the Ice Maiden. Although the road to Elmar was now a good one and the journey might take only a few days they progressed slowly on account of Mrs Trotter's age and her being unused to travelling so far. It was, as she said, her great adventure. 'And I want to enjoy every part of it, my dear,' she told her husband as she made ready to depart.

They crossed the Waste Plains without incident and at last wound their way into the mountains of Cadaelin. These mountains were now safe to pass since the days when Oswain had first struggled through them to reach the Great Forest and although it was cold in the high passes the views were spectacular. To the east they could make out the misty swathes of the Great Forest and to the west lay the glinting towers of Elmar. Descending the mountains they were now within striking distance of the city and, in spite of the serious message that they carried, both were excited at the thought of visiting Oswain's home place and meeting the King and the Queen. Although a cool wind had blown up from the south the day itself was fine and it drew to a close with a glorious sunset.

'Well, we'll reach the city tomorrow, that's for sure,' said Stiggle.

'I think I shall be glad to arrive,' Mrs Trotter answered. 'I've enjoyed the change of scenery and the views from the mountains were really wonderful, but I have to admit my old bones are beginning to feel tired.'

Stiggle laughed. 'You have done far better than many of twice your age,' he said.

'Well, I don't mind a bit of flattery now and again, so I'll thank you for the compliment, kind sir!' she replied.

They were rounding a gentle curve in the road and ahead on the right stood a small copse of trees whose tops burned gold in the last rays of the dying sun. Suddenly, they heard a noise like the splintering of ice.

'Hm, I wonder what that was?' said Stiggle.

Mrs Trotter shook her head. 'It sounded almost like something falling through the trees,' she said.

They reached the copse and thought that they would probably stay there for the night, when they heard a woman's voice calling.

'Help me! Help me, please help me.'

'It's coming from in the trees,' said Stiggle.

'We had best go and see what we can do, if somebody needs us,' said Mrs Trotter, and with that they scurried off the road and into the woodland.

It took the badger and the weasel very little time to find the woman. There laying in a tangle of broken branches and with her face twisted in pain was a woman of middle age and dressed in a russet-coloured travelling cloak.

'Oh, thank goodness someone has come, please help me,' she gasped when she saw them. 'I am hurt.'

Mrs Trotter and Stiggle, their faces full of concern scurried across to where she lay.

'What's wrong, my dear?' asked Mrs Trotter. 'Where are you injured?'

'I'm not sure,' said the woman. 'It seems to be all over; everything hurts.'

'What happened?' asked Stiggle looking around him and trying to work out what had put the woman in such distress.

'I . . . er, I fell. I . . . I fell from the tree,' she groaned.

'What were you doing up the tree?'

'I had become lost,' she gasped, 'and I thought I would climb the tree to find my way back to the road but . . . but I slipped and I fell.' She looked at them hopefully. 'I am so glad you have come, I really thought I might die if nobody turned up. Can you help me?' her eyes settled on Stiggle. 'Oh please, please can you help me?' she begged.

Stiggle seemed particularly moved by the woman's plight. 'Of course we can, and of course we will,' he said. He snuffled at the woman's cloak and stroked her with his paw. Then he turned to Mrs Trotter.

'Quickly, we must give her some water and what food we have so that she can regain her strength.' Then turning to the woman, he said gently, 'I think you should rest here for the time being, and we'll see what we can do in the morning. I don't think we could carry you out of the woods by ourselves. But we are not that far from Elmar and I am sure we can fetch help for you.'

'Oh, thank you,' murmured the woman and her eyes looked softly at Stiggle, which Mrs Trotter found a little disconcerting.

'Yes, well, we will stay with you for the night,' she said,

unpacking some food from her knapsack. 'Indeed, we were planning to rest here for the night ourselves so we may as well keep you company until the morning.'

'That would be very nice,' said the woman. 'I think that I am beginning to feel a little better already, but I know that I cannot walk. My legs seem to be injured.'

'Well, it won't be a bad night,' said Stiggle, 'and we will snuggle up close to you to keep you warm.'

'Thank you, my dear,' said the woman. 'Oh, and we have not introduced ourselves. What are your names?'

'I am Mrs Trotter,' said the badger.

'And I am Stiggle,' said the weasel.

'Well, Stiggle, what a fine name for a fine creature.' Her eyes were soft as she looked at him. 'My name is Kara,' she said.

'Kara, it is a lovely name,' Stiggle answered. 'It suits you.'

'Well, we must get ourselves comfortable,' said Mrs Trotter bustling around and clearing a patch on the ground so that she could lie down in comfort.

'Aren't you going to snuggle up to Kara?' asked Stiggle.

'I don't think so,' said Mrs Trotter. 'I will be more comfortable here, I suspect.'

'But you will keep me warm, won't you Stiggle?' said the woman. She struggled to a sitting position so that her back leaned against the trunk of the tree from which she said she had fallen. She patted the ground and invited the weasel closer.

Mrs Trotter's mind felt uneasy as she settled down to rest, and she whispered a little prayer to Elmesh, not only for her husband and all her friends but for safety and protection during the night. Stiggle meanwhile, snuggled up close to the woman.

Night came early in the woodlands and exhausted by her travels Mrs Trotter was soon fast asleep. The woman, Kara, reached into her cloak and drew out a small lyre. Stiggle looked with interest. She smiled down at him, a kindly smile that made him feel very warm inside. Then she began to pluck on her lyre. Her fingers were nimble and the gentle rhythm and sweet melody soon had the weasel totally entranced.

He forgot about his travels and adventures and the purpose of his mission to Elmar. All he could see was the woman, all he could hear was her music, and all he could smell was the attractive smell of her cloak.

How long into the night it was he couldn't say but at length the woman stopped her playing. Mesmerised he glanced at her face. It was no longer the face of a woman but that of a very, very attractive lady weasel.

She bent down and rubbed her nose against his. 'You must let me ride on your back,' she whispered. 'You must take me to Elmar, and do so now, at once. There must be no delay, but I cannot walk.'

Stiggle nodded his head and purred quietly. 'Of course I will,' he said. 'It will be my honour and privilege.'

Very quietly she climbed on his back and without waking Mrs Trotter, Stiggle slunk off through the woods and onto the open road.

'You are a fine, strong creature,' whispered Kara. 'Such firm shoulders, such a smooth body, such powerful legs, too. Bear me swiftly my love, bear me swiftly to Elmar for I have work to do and it must be done before the night is over.'

Stiggle, in spite of the weariness of the day, felt a new strength in his muscles, and he began to run steadily along the road to where the sleeping city of Elmar lay not many miles distant.

They reached the outskirts of the city sometime in the early hours of the morning before it was light and while the city gates were still closed and guarded.

'We will have to ask the guards for permission to enter,' said Stiggle as they came in sight of the gates.

'That will present no problem,' said Kara softly.

These being days of peace in Elmar only a light guard was posted; it consisted of two soldiers, and they were not armed. Stiggle and his burden reached the gates and he was about to ask for permission to enter when he heard music, and suddenly the load lifted from his shoulders. He glanced over his shoulder and saw the woman, standing before him and playing her lyre. Without a word being spoken, the guards silently opened the gates, and she passed through leaving a bewildered but still mesmerised Stiggle to follow her, sniffing at her trailing cloak.

For the rest of that night they wandered the streets of Elmar while she played her lyre rhythmically and sweetly; and all over Elmar children woke and silently slipped from their beds and from their rooms and from their homes and began to follow the lady and her music. Before long, every child in Elmar had joined a great crocodile that wound through the streets, following the lady and the bemused Stiggle, until they passed from the city and into the open countryside.

Mrs Trotter woke with the first rays of the sun filtering through the trees. She sniffed the morning air and looked around. To her surprise and consternation Stiggle and the woman were nowhere to be seen. *Something is wrong*, she thought to herself. *My bones may be old but they still have their feelings. Something is wrong!* With that, she scuttled out from the shelter of the woodland and onto the road as fast as her legs could carry her. Glancing each way she started on her journey to cover the last few miles to Elmar hoping and praying that Stiggle was all right.

She reached the city gates to find the whole place in commotion. It being her first time in a city, she wondered if this was how it always was, for people were running this way and that, shouting and crying and calling. Men looked angry and women distraught and names were being called – names of children and loved ones – and guards were everywhere and horses were wheeling and charging out of the gates and the dust was rising, and Mrs Trotter began to wish she had not made the journey after all.

Nobody stopped her as she entered the gate and she had no idea which direction to go. In the end she asked a young man the way to the palace.

'The palace?' said the man. 'It's straight down the main highway until you come to the centre of the town by the river. But nobody will have time to see you in the palace.'

'Why is that?' she asked.

'The city is in uproar. It's the children. They've all disappeared,' he explained.

Mrs Trotter furrowed her brow. 'Then I must speak with the King and Queen as soon as possible. I think I can help,' she said.

'You, how can you help?' he asked.

'That I must tell them,' said Mrs Trotter. 'Is there some way you could help me get to the palace quickly, do you think?'

'Well, er, I suppose I could. I've been trying to help

others find their children. Um, I don't have any of my own as yet, so yes. All right.'

With that he picked up the badger and began to run down the main highway towards the palace.

The palace steps were guarded by soldiers and as the young man lowered the badger to the ground, they asked him to state his business. Mrs Trotter said who she was and that she had come on a matter of great urgency.

'There's no time for anyone to see you today,' said the soldier. 'We have orders not to disturb the King and the Queen – or the Princess. As you will realise they have much on their minds at the moment with the disappearance of all the children. I'm afraid you must wait until tomorrow.'

'But this won't wait,' said Mrs Trotter. 'I have news that may help to find your children.'

'I'm sorry,' said the soldier. 'I have my orders.'

Mrs Trotter was just wondering what to do when she heard a cry. She glanced up, her whiskers twitching expectantly. 'Why,' she breathed. 'I believe I have my answer.'

Running down the palace steps was none other than Princess Alena, whom Mrs Trotter had met before.

'Mrs Trotter,' cried Princess Alena. 'Mrs Trotter, what are you doing here? How wonderful to see you. Please come in at once.'

The guard stood aside and Mrs Trotter after thanking the young man for his assistance accompanied Princess Alena into the palace.

'It's wonderful to see you,' said Princess Alena. 'But sadly, you find us at a very difficult time.'

'I know,' said Mrs Trotter. 'Something about all the children disappearing? That is most strange and terrible.'

'It's terrible because no one can find the children. We've had horsemen riding out searching the roads but so far nobody has discovered a thing.'

'I have some news, which may help,' said Mrs Trotter.

'News! Oh, that's good. You must come and meet father and mother at once. They will be very pleased to see you, and very interested in your news. Does it come from my brother, Oswain?'

'I do have some news from Oswain, but I have something else, too,' Mrs Trotter replied.

She was ushered into the royal courtroom where much fuss was made of her as soon as Princess Alena introduced her.

'We are very, very honoured to meet you,' said the King. 'Your courage and loyalty are well known to us here in Elmar and had we had more time we would have arranged a much better welcome for you than this. However, I am afraid to say, we are in a crisis.'

Queen Talesanna looked at Mrs Trotter curiously. 'You bring news,' she said. 'News of great importance that you have brought from Oswain, but other news too, I think.'

'Your wisdom is well known, your highness,' said Mrs Trotter. 'I can see little escapes you. Yes, I have news. . . .'

Mrs Trotter recounted all that had happened in the Great Forest including the cold and the news from Wheezer and Horatio about the penguins. She also told of Oswain's vision of the idol and of their plans to travel to the island of Aethius. At this the King and Queen glanced at one another.

'It was a long time ago now,' said the King. 'At the time of the Great Unrest. We fought a great and successful campaign against the one whom we do not name, but must name again, against Shugob the Devourer. We banished him from Caris Meriac. Does this signal him seeking to break in again?'

'We must prepare for that possibility,' said Queen Talesanna. She turned to Mrs Trotter. 'What is your other news?' she asked. 'For I can tell that you are agitated.'

Mrs Trotter recounted her journey and how she and Stiggle had met the woman. 'I didn't like her one bit,' she said. 'I kept my distance. But she seemed to have some hold over Stiggle. The trouble was, I'm afraid, I was so weary that I soon fell asleep. Just one thing I do recall, though,' she added. 'I thought I could hear music. Strange that.'

Queen Talesanna leaned forwards. 'Mrs Trotter,' she asked. 'How was this woman dressed, what did she call herself, and especially, what kind of music was it that you heard?'

'Your first question is easy,' the badger replied. 'She wore a russet cloak, a very lovely fur cloak, I thought. The second is easy, too. She introduced herself as Kara. As to the third, I'm not so sure. It wasn't a pipe . . . more like strings being plucked. Something like a harp, maybe.'

'As I thought,' said the Queen. She turned to her husband and her face was grim. 'She's back. The name has changed but the Liar has returned, and she has brought her lyre with her!'

11

The Rescue

Oswain bounded across the floor of the cave. Even as he did so, Sarah was whisked into the air, struggling and kicking for all she was worth. An enormous tussle seemed to be taking place. Then the orange glow faded like a switched-off floodlight and to the amazement of those who watched she floated towards them with no more strength than a leaf carried helplessly on the breeze.

For a moment the shocked onlookers thought this was some fresh madness on her part, and Wheezer for one was on the verge of making a quick exit. Crazy girls who could fly without wings were all too much for him! Then the air around her began to glow a soft pink, and Oswain, for one, understood what was happening.

Seconds later the Ice Maiden became visible again and stood before them, somewhat grim-faced and clutching a struggling Sarah in her arms. Oswain made to help her.

'Do not touch her,' cautioned Loriana. 'Much evil still rests upon her!' With that, she dragged the protesting child away towards the tunnel entrance. The others drew back in awe.

The Ice Maiden moved with the swift strides of a determined woman and they had to follow her as best they could. Soon they were deep inside the tunnel, and by the pink glow which she radiated could see she had stopped

at one of the wider places where there was space to stand
together.

Peter looked at his sister with a mixture of fear and
wonder. She now lay sullen at their feet, breathing with a
deep snarl which curled her lip quite frightfully. He
turned tearfully to the Ice Maiden.

'Can you help her?' he began. 'I mean . . . we thought
she . . . it . . . had beaten you. Her . . . her power seemed
greater . . . ,' he stammered.

Loriana smiled gently upon him. 'Peter, do not believe
all you have heard concerning evil. False light never yet
overcame those who possess the true light – nor will it
ever. Things may appear to go badly for a while, but do
not doubt the final outcome. There really is no power to
match the love of Elmesh!'

She turned to Oswain. 'The battle is not lost, my love,
nor is Sarah's suffering in vain. Through this conflict I
have learned a lot about the nature of our enemies. They
tried to reach me through Sarah, until I chose to cloak
myself in light and become invisible to them – and appar-
ently to you also,' she smiled.

'Are you going to sing to her? Is she hypnotised?'
Andrew remembered the power of the Ice Maiden's song
from their previous adventures.

'She is not so much hypnotised as, I think, drugged,'
replied Loriana. 'Though the effects are similar.'

'Sa!' exclaimed Rag suddenly. 'Sa!'

'Sa?' repeated Oswain. 'What is that?'

'She made drink Sa,' said the boy. 'So she do what Stribs
say.'

'Is that what the drug is called?' Peter asked.

Rag nodded eagerly. Andrew was just about to ask if

there was a cure when their new-found friend made a dive for him and grabbed at his belt. Then, beaming with triumph, he began to dance about waving a small sprig of leaves. For a moment everyone was startled by this strange behaviour.

'These make better,' he grinned. 'They make me better when I drink Sa.'

Oswain laughed out loud with amazement. 'Rag, you are a most useful chap to have around! Not only a faithful guide but a medicine man as well. So your fall was not in vain after all, Andrew. These leaves must have caught on you when you landed on the shrub. Elmesh is with us indeed!'

Andrew smiled ruefully, but felt better for knowing that there was some good purpose behind his accident. He wondered if it were always so.

Loriana took the leaves and knelt beside Sarah. As soon as the girl saw them she cried out in distress and held up her hands to protect her face.

'No, poison! I am a Strib! I must not taste this. It is bad for me. I will obey Lord Yarx.'

She twisted her head this way and that and backed up against the wall, refusing to allow the leaves near her mouth. Peter made to grab hold of her head but Loriana looked up at him sharply. 'Your care does you credit, Peter, but I said do not touch her if you want to remain unharmed yourself.' Peter blushed and withdrew.

Oswain gave him a reassuring smile and put his hand on his shoulder. Then they heard the Ice Maiden begin to sing.

She sang of forests fair; of birds and trees and running waters brightly sparkling; moist mosses, green meadows and flowering carpets – gold, red, violet and cheerful yellow. Her song stretched to shady woods where soft paths lay brown, inviting, wending to where fishes sported in cool meres, and on to dappled glades and secret places for passing happy summer hours.

Oswain's heart rose with longing for the Great Forest that he loved so well. He thought of his chief advisors, Trotter and Stiggle, of Fumble, Mumble and Grumble, his faithful retainers whose antics still brought smiles to the faces of all those who knew them. He recalled the enchanted glade and the glory of the Merestone that radiated such life and blessing on his realm.

Sarah, calmed by the magic of the song, allowed the leaf to pass between her lips. They watched anxiously as she began to chew it.

Sweat broke out on her forehead and she grew pale, muttering, frothing a little at the mouth. 'Shugob . . . Shug . . . gob . . . gob . . . gob . . .' she twitched a few times, and then was still.

Her eyes opened wide and for a long moment she looked silently around her.

'Loriana?' she said at last. 'Oswain? Where am I? What's happened to me?' She looked frightened.

'You've been away, Sarah, but you have come back,' said the Ice Maiden soothingly. She laid a hand on the girl's arm.

'I've been a long way away,' Sarah said seriously looking up with large eyes. 'It's been a long journey. I was a stranger and I lost myself.'

'What did you do while you were away?' Oswain asked anxiously.

'I made the Key,' she replied. 'It's an evil key. Oh,

Oswain, I'm so sorry. I didn't mean to do it.' She burst into tears and Oswain moved to comfort her.

'It was not your fault, Sarah,' he said. 'You were drugged and controlled by evil forces. What's done is done and we have you back with us. That is the important thing.'

She relaxed a little and smiled. 'It's wonderful to see you again. I knew we'd meet you somehow. We just didn't know where.'

With that she was more her old self again and soon they were bringing her up to date with the news of all that had happened to them so far.

'I will tell you later about what I have discovered,' said Loriana. 'But I say now that we are faced with the greatest foes we have yet met, and will need to be wise if we are to defeat them. First we must escape from here as quickly as possible.'

'But how?' Peter asked.

'I don't want to go back the way we came,' Andrew said.

'Rag, do you know any other paths from here which do not take us on cliff edges or past dragons?' Oswain asked.

The boy put his hand to his forehead and thought for a moment. 'I know path but Stribs guard it. They see us and fight. It lead back to jungle.'

'Then we'll take it!' Oswain spoke grimly and a light was in his eye. He unsheathed his sword. The blade hissed from the scabbard and glowed faintly in the gloom. 'Lead on, Rag!' he commanded.

The company retraced their steps to the Stribs' main cavern. It was echoingly empty as they clambered to the floor and skirted the walls. Rag was in front, followed closely by Oswain. Then came Peter, Andrew and Wheezer. Loriana brought up the rear holding Sarah's hand.

'So far, so good,' breathed Oswain.

They turned into a long ice tunnel, lit like the rest by crystals hanging on the wall. At the far end it forked left and right. Rag put his finger to his lips and indicated with his other hand that they had to take the left fork and there they would find the guards. Oswain nodded.

Soon they reached the turning. Rag lay on his stomach and peeped round the corner. He held up four fingers to indicate how many guards there were.

'Surprise is our best weapon,' Oswain whispered. 'We'll charge straight through them. Are you ready?'

They nodded.

'Then let's go!'

With that the company swept round the corner and were on the unprepared guards before they knew it. It worked, and the Stribs fell to the floor in complete disarray as six people and a pelican charged through them. By the time they had struggled to their feet, Oswain and his friends were well on their way. Somewhere behind a shrill alarm sounded.

'Well done, everyone,' Oswain panted as they ran.

'Didn't know what hit them,' Andrew laughed. 'Easy!'

However, his jubilation was cut short, for as they ran past another tunnel on their left, they heard a loud cry.

'Halt! This is a Strib order which must be obeyed!'

Moments later, a large troop of Stribs swept from the tunnel to pursue them.

'How much further, Rag?' Oswain called.

'Not far now. They not come into jungle,' he puffed.

A spear flew over their heads and struck their path in a clatter of splintered ice. It was swiftly followed by another, and another.

'Go on ahead, all of you,' Oswain yelled. 'I'll deal with this.'

Sword drawn, he turned to face the oncoming Stribs. His menacing appearance halted them in their tracks, but the spears continued to fly at him. His blade flashed in the crystal light, faster than the eye could follow shattering spear after spear with his swishing strokes. More and more Stribs flooded into the tunnel; more and more spears flew through the air.

Oswain glanced over his shoulder. His companions had all escaped.

'That's enough of this,' he muttered, and slowly he withdrew down the tunnel, still fending off the hail of weapons.

He passed from the ice, through the slush and on to firm rock, and then there was light at the end of the tunnel. His pursuers began to lose heart and, when the air grew warm, gave up the attack, chanting instead, 'Surrender. This is a Strib order which must be obeyed.' Oswain turned and ran into the open air.

'Over here, Oswain,' Peter called.

He looked up to see the others standing on the hillside above the cave mouth. The children cheered and the Ice Maiden clapped her hands. Wheezer cawed with delight.

'Well, we're free and together,' Oswain laughed as he joined them. 'That's something. Well done, Rag – and everyone.'

Just as he spoke, the air was rent by an horrendous roar that shook the ground under their feet and echoed off the hills like thunder. The branches of the trees clattered as thousands of birds took fright and flew screeching from their nests.

'Mmm, we do seem to have started something,' murmured the Ice Maiden.

12

Mrs Trotter Follows the Scent

'You have brought us serious news, indeed,' said King Argil. 'If she is whom we suspect then she is likely to be behind the mischief that has fallen upon us today.'

'It is incredible that she should dare to come to Elmar again,' said the Queen. 'Such barefaced arrogance!'

'She must feel very sure of herself,' Princess Alena observed. 'It means she is not alone.'

'I have a terrible thought,' whispered Queen Talesanna. 'The children! She could be in league with Shugob himself.'

'If so, then Oswain and Loriana are facing a terrible foe,' said the King. 'Perhaps worse than in my day.'

Mrs Trotter listened to all this with patience but then interrupted. 'But who is she? Who is this woman and why is she so dangerous?'

'Forgive me,' said the Queen turning to her. 'We have been poor hosts and you do not know what is happening. This woman – she was known by a different name when last she came to our city. Then she was called Kinera. She arrived one day during the years of the Great Unrest that followed the defeat of Shugob. We did not know she was evil at the time. Many people pass through this city and because it has always been a place of beauty and art we are for ever welcoming painters and sculptors and actors – and musicians.'

'I was too young to remember her,' said Princess Alena, 'but was she not a wonderful lyre player?'

'Outstanding, outstanding,' said the King. 'Beautiful in a strange way, too; full of subtle grace in the way she moved. And such nimble fingers when she played.'

'My husband was most impressed!' said the Queen, her laugh breaking their seriousness for a moment.

'Sadly, I was wrong,' said King Argil. 'Her gracefulness concealed malice. It was all a lie. You see, her real purpose was to snare Oswain.'

'I could see that much,' Queen Talesanna continued. 'But Oswain was in love with someone whom you later met in her corrupted form, Mrs Trotter.'

'You mean Hagbane – Dorinda as she was then.'

'Indeed. Oswain, of course, had eyes for no one else and when Kinera saw that she had no chance with him, she grew spiteful. She befriended Dorinda and planted the seeds of evil in her heart. I don't know how many lies and deceits she told, but, well, the rest you know, for you in the Great Forest were victims of that same deceit.'

'The evil behind the evil. I've always said bad apples make more bad apples,' said Mrs Trotter.

'Truly,' nodded the King. 'Well, that will have to do for the moment. You have brought us bad news but news that may help us solve the mystery of why the children have disappeared.'

'I may be able to do more than that,' Mrs Trotter replied. 'I may be able to find them.'

At this all eyes fixed on her.

'It's this woman's cloak.'

'Ah, yes, she wore it back then,' said the Queen. 'The colour of a golden weasel of the trees.'

'I didn't like it,' said Mrs Trotter. 'It was made from animal fur, after all. My travelling companion did, though. The thing is, it had a definite smell about it. If I could pick up the scent it might lead us to her and to the children.'

'Brilliant!' cried Princess Alena. 'Where do you want to start?'

'I'll call for the guards to accompany you,' said the King.

It was agreed that Mrs Trotter should be taken outside the city gates, since there was nowhere so many children could still remain secreted in the city itself and the scent would be lost by now, anyway. They soon found that the road was no use either because too many people were coming and going. In any case, the road had been searched for many miles without success.

'Leave me to search by myself, otherwise you will confuse my snout,' said Mrs Trotter. 'Too many smells spoil the scent, you understand.'

Mrs Trotter began her search two hundred metres along the wall from the gates and set out in a semicircle that would bring her back to the same distance on the other side of the gates. It took a long time as she patiently snuffled the ground and the twigs and branches for any hint that the woman had passed this way.

At length, she reached the wall again, her half circle completed. There was nothing.

Mrs Trotter was not one to give up. Although her paws ached and she wanted nothing more than to lie down in the shade, she began to snuffle along the walls, prepared if necessary to track all the way round the city. *If they didn't go through the gates then they must have gone over the walls*, she said to herself.

After two more weary hours she was only a quarter of the way around the city and on the point of giving up when she came to what she was looking for. A dry but deep and overgrown culvert ran under the city walls and there she picked up the scent.

'So that's how she did it,' she murmured. 'Not over, but under.'

Climbing down into the culvert, she scurried along, picking up not just the scent of the woman but also that of Stiggle and of many children. There were other signs that people had passed this way: footprints in the softer earth, broken twigs on shrubs. The heat of the chase made her forget everything else, including what she would do when she found her quarry.

Suddenly, she was there. The rainwater culvert led to a wooded part of the river and on the bank stood hidden by the trees hundreds and hundreds of children, all of them silent and still. Puffing and panting, Mrs Trotter came to a stop. She could hear music, lyre music carried on the afternoon air.

'Well, at least I'll know where to find her,' she said to herself.

The woman was standing by the riverside playing her lyre, and there was Stiggle beside her fawning at her cloak and gazing longingly into her face. Mrs Trotter's whiskers twitched with annoyance. 'Fat lot of help he's going to be,' she said. 'I'll just have to tackle her myself, that's all.'

She looked around and her eyes caught sight of something on the river, or rather several things, though she was unsure of what they were. Drifting slowly upstream were a number of crystalline pyramids, their sides gleaming silver in the afternoon light. Whatever they were, Mrs

Trotter sensed that she had to deal with the lyre player before they reached the children. She scurried forward as fast as her short legs could carry her.

'Ah, we meet again. How delightful,' said the woman as Mrs Trotter arrived on the scene. She continued her playing without interruption. 'You must be very eager to join us for I can see that you are covered in dust and very tired. Then, I do understand, for most creatures find my company attractive. Like Stiggle here; he finds me irresistible, don't you, Stiggle dear?'

Stiggle gave something that sounded like a mew and rubbed the side of his head against her cloak.

'Do you want to join him? I'm sure you do,' said the woman sweetly.

'Why have you taken all these children?' Mrs Trotter demanded. She was not going to fall for the woman's smooth tongue.

Kinera, or Kara as she presently called herself, opened her eyes wide in disbelief. 'I have taken no children,' she said. 'Why, you make me sound like a common thief. These dear children have followed me of their own accord. Do you really think that I could single-handed, or even with the aid of dear Stiggle here, kidnap a city full of children?' She laughed lightly.

'Then why are they here?' Mrs Trotter insisted.

'They have responded to an invitation, a generous offer on my part. I am giving them a free holiday by the sea, and it will cost neither them nor their parents a single coin.' She cocked her head to one side. 'Would you like to come with us as well? I have even arranged for transport so that everyone can rest their legs.'

For a moment Mrs Trotter was nonplussed. Then she

recalled what she had been told at the palace. 'I don't believe you,' she ventured. 'This isn't the first time you've been to this city from what I hear and you caused mischief last time. I think you are doing the same again.'

A flicker of anger flashed across the woman's face. 'You should not believe all you hear,' she replied. 'It is true that they do not like me in the palace. They were jealous of my beauty and of my skill on the lyre. I had to leave because the pain was too great.' A tear formed in her eye and ran down her cheek. 'They were too cruel to me.'

'Why then did you return?' demanded Mrs Trotter.

'Why? Because I am a kind-hearted and forgiving woman, and a sentimental fool, I suppose. I really liked the people of this city and I thought I would return for old times' sake. So I wandered the streets playing my lyre and thinking of the good times that I had before everyone turned against me. These children – so different from the grown ups – listened to me and they came out to make me welcome. I feel so happy again and I wanted to reward them for their kindness, so I have arranged this little trip for them.'

'I want to ask them for themselves,' said Mrs Trotter. 'Stop playing that music, will you?'

Kinera's face hardened. 'You don't believe me. You think I am lying,' she said. 'I can see they have twisted your mind, just like the others.'

Mrs Trotter had been coming ever closer to the woman. 'If you are telling the truth then you have nothing to hide,' she said in her most reasonable voice. 'These will confirm your words, but you must stop playing so they can speak.'

Very gently she reached up a paw and laid it across the lyre strings, damping the sound.

The woman snarled with rage and with a hissing and a spitting she in a moment altered in shape. Mrs Trotter, flung back by the force of the change, found herself confronting a fierce and very large golden weasel that wasted no time, but leapt upon her seeking her throat.

For a moment Mrs Trotter was caught off guard and she might have been killed by the fierceness of the attack. Maybe it was because she was indignant about the way the woman had lied to her, or maybe it was because she now knew that the woman's deceit lay deep behind the sufferings that had fallen upon the Great Forest, whatever the reason, sudden anger lent her strength and she threw off the weasel with a surprising ease.

Having lost the advantage of surprise, the weasel now confronted Mrs Trotter warily her teeth bared and her sinuous body preparing for another attack. Mrs Trotter squared her shoulders and bared her claws. She had no intention of losing this battle. *Best defence is to attack*, she thought, and with that she leapt into the fray, dealing the weasel a resounding blow to the head that sent her spinning across the ground.

Encouraged by her success Mrs Trotter waded in again, but just as her confidence was growing, she heard a snarl behind her. Whirling round she saw to her dismay that another weasel was coming for her.

'Stiggle!' she gasped. 'It's me! What are you doing?'

The mesmerised weasel seemed not to hear her but reared up for a fight. Overwhelmed for a moment, Mrs Trotter was not to be outdone. 'I can see I'll have to knock some sense into you,' she gasped. 'I remember when you were born, you young whippersnapper. Have more respect for your elders and betters or I'll speak with your mother!' With that she cuffed the weasel twice around the head, but she withdrew her claws as she did so.

Stiggle staggered back, but Kinera was on her feet again. She was wounded and blood ran down her face, for Mrs Trotter had used her claws to good effect. Rage filled her eyes. 'She has harmed me, Stiggle, my love. Help me,' she cried.

Mrs Trotter knew she was in trouble. An old badger might take on one weasel, but two was more than she could handle. Nor could she hope to outrun them – and that would still leave the children. Out of the corner of her eye she could see them milling around. Without the woman's music the spell was wearing off and they were growing restless. Maybe that was her one hope.

'Help me! Help me!' she cried.

Her calls and the general commotion caught the attention of some of the children and seeing the badger outnumbered one or two picked up stones and began to fling them at the two weasels. It gave Mrs Trotter the breathing space she needed.

'Run! Run for the city!' she shouted. 'Enemies are here!'

Slowly, the message caught on and the children began to turn towards Elmar but nobody seemed to be in a hurry. What Mrs Trotter wanted was a panic. 'Soul Wolves!' she cried. 'Child-eaters! Flee! Run for your lives!'

It worked. Somewhere in the melee a child screamed. Others joined in and the next minute they were surging in a noisy mass towards the safety of the city.

Kinera now had a problem. If she remained in the form of a weasel she would lose the children but if she turned back into a woman the badger would live. Mrs Trotter had her own ideas. Ignoring her peril she turned away from the fleeing children and ran towards the two weasels, but instead of attacking them she ran around them. Lying on the grass was Kinera's lyre and Mrs Trotter made straight for it. She seized it in her jaws and ran to the riverside where with all the strength she could muster, she flung it into the water. To her dismay, it did not sink but nonetheless it began to drift steadily downstream.

Kinera howled with rage as she saw what had happened and ignoring both the children and Mrs Trotter she ran to the water's edge and dived in. The last the badger saw of her was her swimming as fast as she could after her rapidly disappearing lyre, though whether it was as a golden weasel or a woman, she couldn't say.

With a satisfied smile Mrs Trotter dusted her paws and turned. 'Now to sort you out, my lad!' she said to a rather dejected looking Stiggle.

* * *

The story of Mrs Trotter's heroism was soon the talk of the town with the criers everywhere announcing: *Lady Trotter saves the children! Courageous badger outwits cunning foe! Bold badger battles slinky sneaky siren!*

The palace was delighted and everyone stood when that evening, leaning on the arm of the King himself, she was escorted into a banquet held in her honour. She sat between the King and Princess Alena.

'My, my, this is one up on my dear husband,' she said. 'Just wait until he hears about this!'

'Oh, he will hear soon enough,' Princess Alena laughed. 'You'll be the talk of the Great Forest, too.'

'Well, I don't want to make too much of it, my dear,' Mrs Trotter answered. 'Can't have these things going to my head at my age.'

'Well, whatever you say, you saved the day and all the people of Elmar are grateful to you.' She leaned across Mrs Trotter. 'Isn't that right, father?'

'Oh, what? Er, yes. Yes, absolutely, my dear,' said the King. 'Wonderful. Wonderful. It will go down in the official chronicles.'

Only one person was less than happy on this festive occasion. Poor Stiggle had come to his senses soon enough once Kinera had fled and he had been horrified when Mrs Trotter told him what he had done. 'You really are very silly,' she scolded him. 'It was your job to protect me, not the other way round. Since when was I the commander-in-chief?'

The hapless weasel had offered his apologies and Mrs Trotter had forgiven him. 'There's only one thing for it,' she said. 'We must look out an attractive lady weasel for you when we return to the forest. Otherwise there's no knowing who else will turn your head!'

Talking of heads, Stiggle had excused himself from the banquet on the grounds that his head ached from Mrs Trotter's cuffing, but mostly, if the truth be told, he was too ashamed of his conduct to be seen in public. Nursing his sore head he sat in his room dreading what Oswain and Trotter would say when he returned to the Great Forest.

While all this was going on the royal guards were searching everywhere for Kinera and everyone had been warned to be on the look out, and to be careful about what music they listened to. But, the woman with the russet cloak had disappeared into thin air along with the floating pyramids that Mrs Trotter had seen, and nobody was the wiser as to why or what she had planned to do with the children.

13
The Image of Shugob

While all these events were taking place, Lord Yarx hovered in a trance before the Image of Shugob.

It was a monstrous idol, with its bloated amber body and its squat, heavily creased face scowling across the frozen hillsides. Yarx had no idea how it came to be on the island of Aethius, nor did it occur to him to ask, but he had expected to find it here. The subtle voice of Kinera, the Prophetess and lyre player, had told him what to look for as he led the penguins on their fateful journey across the frozen seas.

When they arrived, bearing their stolen burden, Yarx had quickly discovered that Shugob himself spoke from this idol – and spoke only to him. Not even his cronies, Raaz and Kig, had that privilege. They simply obeyed orders, like everyone else.

'I, and I alone, have been chosen for the secret counsels of Shugob the Almighty!' he said. It gave him a feeling of great satisfaction.

Yarx remembered the day that the woman had first arrived. Kara, she called herself, though later she said that her name was Kinera. He recalled her beautiful russet cloak and the sinuous way that she moved as she played on her lyre – so different from any other creature that inhabited the deep cold lands of Caris Meriac. Yarx was captivated. She spoke with him for many weeks. 'You have such strength,' she said. 'Such a fine coat and a noble beak. You are destined to be a great leader. I know what, I will call you Lord Yarx from now on!'

Lord Yarx. He had liked the sound of that.

So it had continued, until the emperor penguin really believed that he would be the greatest leader of them all.

'A leader must lead, and you must take the penguins on a great journey,' she had said. 'For here in the deep south your fame will spread only a little. You must move north, and you must take the South Pole with you. Now that would be a real mark of greatness!'

With the aid of her music, the penguins had wrested the South Pole from its proper setting. It had been a terrible task and many had died, but at last it was done and so began the journey to the island of Aethius.

Once there, she had escorted him to the Image of Shugob and had, by means unknown to him, provided him with the tools to do the idol's bidding. He had seen little of her after that, for she had the ability to come and go at will, as though she inhabited more than one world. Not that he was greatly worried; the Image spoke to him in the same flattering tones and with promises of power and glory.

Yarx smiled in his trance-state before the Image. 'What rewards will be mine! What power!' he mused. 'Lord Yarx the penguin-god. Invincible! No one will ever dare challenge my rule!'

Steady as a statue he waited, drinking in the power of the Image, swallowing the cold-blooded evil that had chilled his heart more than the winds that blew over the frozen southern lands of his native abode. It seemed years ago that he had dwelt there, happy, young and carefree. Now the short months since Kinera and Shugob had corrupted him made those years as nothing and the dim spark of better days faded like an old photograph.

Yarx was interrupted by one of his Strib captains.

'My Lord,' he cried. 'I beg you to forgive my intrusion but terrible news has reached me. The Strib child who made the Key has escaped, and so have the two boys. They have with them a giant who wields a flaming sword. Our spears were no match for him.'

Yarx blinked, then snapped his beak angrily. 'The guards will be severely punished for this. She should have been watched, or returned to the others. Why was this not done?'

The Strib had no answer, so Yarx continued. 'It no longer matters. She has served her purpose. Now that we have the Key, nothing can thwart our glorious plans. Go now. Send for Raaz and Kig to meet me at once in the council chamber.'

The Strib bowed low and hurried to do his master's bidding.

When the three leaders were gathered Yarx spoke.

'I have heard the will of Shugob. We must wait only two days until the stars and the planets are right. Then we release the fire.'

'It is good,' Raaz responded. He addressed Kig. 'Are the children prepared?'

'They are gathered and their instruction is nearly complete – except for the few who escaped.'

'Little worry. In the Great Purpose they are small fry and will not survive long,' Yarx answered coldly. 'It will take only a short time for them to be captured or destroyed. By then such powers will be loosed that we will only have to think them dead and they will be!'

'How goes the Great Channel?' Kig asked.

'It is nearly ready,' replied Raaz, who had been in charge of this operation. 'The Shining Pole is in place and the fiery tube kept clear. The Key has only to be dropped and the elements will unite. The pyramid is prepared.'

'Excellent!' exclaimed Yarx with a smirk of satisfaction. 'Then we await only the signal from the heavens.'

'What about the dragon? He is stirring because he too awaits this hour,' said Kig. 'Are we sure that he will do us no harm?'

Lord Yarx looked upon his underling with scorn. 'Have I not spoken with Shugob himself? Do you think I have not received assurance concerning these things? Tergan the dragon will lend weight to our cause. He too will serve Shugob, and if one as mighty as he will serve then will not all others do likewise?'

* * *

Oswain and his companions, hidden deep in the jungle, were having a conference.

'Loriana, you spoke of things you learned when you rescued Sarah. It's time for you to tell us what you found out,' said Oswain.

The Ice Maiden sat down on a log. The four children squatted round her while Wheezer perched on the branch of a nearby oleander tree. Oswain leaned against its trunk next to him. Loriana eyed them all gravely.

'We were right. It is the return of Shugob,' she said. 'The foulest of creatures is planning to re-enter Caris Meriac and it is being made possible by an old troublemaker, the lyre player, Kinera. There are also other lesser powers involved.'

'No doubt for what they can get for themselves,' interjected Oswain grimly.

'What sort of powers are they? And who is Shugob?' Sarah asked anxiously.

'We have already said something of this to Peter and Andrew,' Oswain answered. 'Shugob the Devourer is an ancient sky-god, a monstrous demon who delights in all forms of evil but especially in the sacrifice of children.'

'I . . . I've seen him,' Sarah said hesitantly. 'It was in a dream, a nightmare. I had it before . . . before we came into your world again.' She turned to her brothers. 'I told you it meant something bad was happening to Oswain and everyone.'

'You said there were others as well . . .' Peter addressed Loriana.

'The carrion spirit, Dug, has aided them,' she answered.

'The vultures . . .' began Wheezer.

'That is so,' answered the Ice Maiden. 'They, with the help of the lyre player, have captured the children and even now watch over them.' She turned to Oswain. 'Do you remember those pyramids in the mist? I believe that is how the children have been transported here. Sira, the spirit behind such pyramids, has lent her powers to that end.'

Rag nodded excitedly. 'Me brought in pyramid thing. I hear music. I go to sleep and then wake up in it with many children like me. We carried over ice by power of big bad birds.' He blushed at what was for him a long speech.

'But why do they want children? Why not grown-ups?' asked Sarah insistently.

The Ice Maiden spoke thoughtfully. 'Sarah, do you remember what it felt like when you were under the power of the drug, Sa? It did not kill you but it made you want to serve Shugob.'

Sarah gave a shudder at the memory.

'I am not fully sure, but I think that is what he is after,' the Ice Maiden continued.

'You mean he doesn't want sacrifices, as in the past, but he wants slaves?' Oswain interjected.

'Yes, I get the feeling that he will make these children his mind-slaves, much as he temporarily did with Sarah. Then he will feed slowly on their spirits until they are hollow on the inside. They'll probably be given all the toys and sweets they want, but no real choice,' she replied.

'They won't even realise what's happening to them,' said Peter with a sudden flash of insight. 'Like hamsters in a cage, happy so long as they've food and drink and a wheel to run round. Except that hamsters can't always get off the wheel and they run until they die of exhaustion,' he added.

'Elmesh made children to be free,' said Oswain. 'Life is more than toys and sweets, as you well know. You were created to love and to choose, to worship and to serve freely— not to be the slaves of a self-centred tyrant.' He was angry and he clenched his fists. 'And already the first victims of Shugob are prisoners on this accursed island.'

'How did you find all this out?' Andrew asked.

The Ice Maiden grimaced. 'It all happened very quickly. When I disappeared from your sight I found myself facing Kinera. It wasn't difficult to read her mind or her intentions. I expected it to be a hard battle but she was distracted as though part of her was busy somewhere else. And – this is strange – I kept seeing a vision of Mrs Trotter, though she was fierce, as I've never before seen her. Whatever, the lyre player fled and I had Sarah in my arms.'

Sarah wiped her hand across her brow. 'Wh-when I was a prisoner, they made me mix things together and . . . oh, I just can't remember what happened . . . but I didn't feel afraid. I felt somehow better, more important,' she said. 'But it was cold, like . . . like a room that was always tidy and you could never do anything you wanted to. Sort of, not quite human,' she finished.

'I don't fancy that much,' said Andrew. He liked living in a messy room.

'I don't understand what all this has got to do with the South Pole being here,' said Peter

'I think I've got something,' Andrew replied. 'Do you remember that chant of the penguins – and the music?'

'Remember it? It went on so long I could hardly forget it!' his brother replied.

> 'When ice and fire shall meet,
> Then earth and sky be one;
> The Lord beneath the earth
> Shall join the Lord above;
> So speaks the Prophetess;
> For us the wealth and fame!'

'Well, what if the South Pole is the ice and this volcano is the fire? Don't you see?' said Andrew waving his hands with excitement. 'They're going to try and join them together. Right here, on this island!'

'Ice and fire meeting. A truly unnatural joining and needing a key of great power to make it possible,' said Oswain. 'Why, if that were to happen . . .'

The Ice Maiden finished the sentence for him.

'. . . then Shugob would find his way into the world.'

'And I made the key for them, ' added Sarah glumly. 'What a mess!'

'What's done is done, Sarah. It's no use fretting over that. It's what we do next that counts,' said the Ice Maiden.

'That's why we're here.' Oswain spoke decisively. 'We must stop them using that key. And we'd better be quick about it!'

14

Save the Children

'What about the dragon?' Andrew asked. 'Is he what they mean by "the Lord below" in their chant?'

'I would say so,' Oswain replied grimly. 'It is not the first time that Shugob and the dragon have formed an alliance. On the last occasion Tergan was very young. From what you tell me now, he has grown into a monster!'

'Whatever his size, the dragon is stirring, and who knows how hungry he might be. We do not have much time,' the Ice Maiden reminded them.

'What are we going to do?' asked Sarah.

'That's easy,' Peter answered. 'We're going to rescue the children, aren't we, Oswain?'

'We are, indeed,' he replied, his face breaking into a sudden smile. 'And that's where you come in, Rag. Can you take us to where they are imprisoned?'

The wild boy nodded with enthusiasm. 'They not far. Round other side of mountain, where it cold. I lead you there.'

Oswain asked how the children were guarded and Rag told him that it was by some of the penguins and perhaps vultures too.

'Then let's wait until dusk before we make our move,' said Oswain.

'I know they're bad, but will we have to kill the penguins?' asked Sarah. 'I'd prefer not to, if we can help it.'

Oswain smiled. 'I have a plan which will, I hope, make that unnecessary.'

The companions spent the afternoon busily plotting, planning, collecting and making what they needed for the rescue attempt. By early evening they were ready, and with Rag taking the lead, they set off through the jungle, travelling anticlockwise round the volcano. The summit was still shrouded from view by the mysterious cloud. Maybe it was their imagination, but Peter, Sarah and Andrew had the eerie feeling that hidden eyes were watching them as they journeyed.

As the jungle thinned out, the air grew cooler. Peter reckoned that even the power of the South Pole had been unable to freeze that part of the island or the sea because of its nearness to Tergan's lair. Although it was good to be at a distance from the dragon, he felt sorry to leave the warmth and shelter of the jungle for the bleak exposed hills that lay before them. He was beginning to feel apprehensive about their rescue bid.

The shadows lengthened as they skirted the cone of the volcano. By now they were clear of the jungle and high enough to watch the sun sinking blood-red over the frozen sea. The ground grew hard and slippery and the children were once again grateful for the boots and furs with which they had been provided when they arrived on the island. Rag, however, seemed to mind neither the heat nor the cold.

He was chattering nineteen to the dozen to Oswain, who learned something of where he had come from. His home was in a village along the north-west coast of the Wester lands over which Oswain's father ruled, a mountainous region with cold winters and long hot summers.

Oswain discovered that Rag had always been allowed to roam at will and had never gone to school but preferred climbing mountains and exploring hidden valleys. He was friends with animals and had learned much about plants and herbs.

Now, sure-footed, he led his friends over the frozen terrain, clambering the icy rocks with ease. Often he had to wait for the other children to catch up.

'Wow! I wish I could get over rocks the way he does,' said Peter.

'Me too,' replied Andrew.

'I wonder how he managed to escape from the penguins?' puffed Sarah as she struggled alongside them.

'Probably just ran for it and no one could catch him up!'

'I'm going to ask him when we next stop.'

They discovered that Rag had woken up early one morning to find himself trapped inside a crystal pyramid along with all the other children of his village. The thin walls proved to be completely unbreakable. 'Then big birds come and we slide across the sea, but not get wet,' he said. 'I not know how they do it.'

At length the pyramid had come to the island of Aethius and there one side had opened to allow the children out.

The moment they emerged, weak and hungry, they were forced to march between two lines of armed penguins. There was nothing the children could do except obey the Stribs and they were taken to a large hollow surrounded on all sides by high cliffs where they were kept prisoners along with many other children.

The company now drew close to that hollow and Rag indicated that they should move more stealthily.

Cautiously, Rag brought them to the very lip of the dell. In what was left of the daylight they could just make out many children seated cross-legged in neat rows, being instructed by one of the Stribs. Faintly, they could hear the words which the children were being taught to chant.

> 'We are one together;
> We are one with Shugob;
> Stribs and Strats
> And children all;
> Mind and spirit make us one;
> All is One.
> We are free!
> We are One with Shugob.'

'Weird!' was all Andrew could whisper.

Oswain glanced up at the darkening sky. There was no sign of the vultures.

'They drink more Sa soon,' hissed Rag. 'I only drink some and spill rest. That's why I not too bad. And I find leaves and eat, so I get better. Then I creep away.' He grinned, showing white teeth in the dark.

'How often do they drink Sa?' asked Loriana.

'Three times every day,' Rag replied.

'So its power doesn't last too long. That's what I hoped.' She drew out her flask and a large bunch of the leaves that had healed Sarah. Then she gave a quiet whistle. Moments later, Wheezer came gliding in to land.

Unfortunately, he didn't fly well in the dark and he crashed straight into Andrew, knocking him flat on his back. There was much coughing and spluttering from the hapless pelican, before he flew off again leaving Andrew soaking wet.

'What on earth!' he began.

Oswain motioned him to be quiet and pointed to the sky. Their friend was already returning. This time Andrew kept well out of the way and much to everyone's relief Wheezer managed to land safely.

He turned to the Ice Maiden and opened his beak. His pouch was full of water. Now Andrew knew why he had got so wet.

Quickly Loriana tore up the leaves and dropped them into the pelican's mouth. Then she added a few drops of cordial from her own flask.

'Go now, Wheezer,' she whispered. 'And may Elmesh be with you!'

With that the bird flew off softly into the night. His friends watched anxiously, straining their eyes through the gloom as he circled the hollow and slowly descended on the far side.

He landed behind a rock, this time with greater care, and peered around.

I wish I could see better, he thought. *Now where do they keep it? Aha!*

He spied an alcove in the rocks, guarded by three strong Stribs with their spears at the ready. Within the alcove burned one of the crystal lights which the Stribs used in their headquarters. *They must be guarding something pretty important*, thought the pelican. *That's my target, I reckon.*

He stretched his large wings and with scarcely a sound glided round until he was perched on a buttress of rock above the Strib guards. He glanced down. There, sure enough, gleamed a tub of liquid and next to it a number of stone cups.

Now, how do I get to it without being spotted? he wondered. *What I need is a distraction.*

He pondered for a moment and had an idea. There were some loose stones on the ledge where he stood. He began to push at them. At first, they wouldn't budge because of the ice. Then they loosened and he kicked several off the ledge. The stones fell with a loud clatter to the right of the Stribs. Swiftly, he took to the air and began to caw loudly over the spot where they had fallen, as though he was injured.

The effect on the guards was immediate. They were on the alert, peering through the gloom at the noise. One started forward, half-followed by another.

Wheezer could hear them speaking.

'What was that?'

'I don't know but we must not leave the Sa. It is a Strat order which must be obeyed.'

'But it may be an attack. We should investigate.'

While the guards were preoccupied with what to do and looking the wrong way, Wheezer seized his chance. He glided noiselessly down on to the rim of the tub. Then, stooping as if to drink, he quietly let the potion in his mouth run into the Sa.

He was only just in time. The Stribs decided not to investigate the disturbance and one turned just as Wheezer flew off.

With a harsh cry the guard threw his spear at the bird. Fortunately, it missed and shattered harmlessly against the rock. In a moment Wheezer was gone. He glanced back to see the Stribs huddled around the tub. They seemed relieved that it had not been overturned. He grinned to himself and found a perch out of harm's way in the dark.

From there he watched with satisfaction as the children were lined up and marched like zombies to the tub. Each was given a cup full of Sa.

So far so good, he thought. *Let's hope the Ice Maiden's potion works*. As silently as he had come he flew back to rejoin his companions.

'How long will we have to give it?' Peter whispered to Oswain.

'About an hour, I expect,' he answered. 'The medicine will work quite speedily.'

That hour seemed to take ages, and by the end of it they were feeling very cramped and stiff. At last Loriana gave the signal for the second part of their rescue plan.

Oswain unfurled a large bundle which he had been carrying. It consisted of the afternoon's work – several rope ladders made from long creepers of the kind they had used to rescue Andrew when he fell.

The first of these ladders was quietly unrolled and lowered from the edge of the cliff. Rag slipped silently over and clambered swiftly to its base, vanishing into the gloom.

For a while nothing happened, then suddenly the silence was broken by Rag running into the open and shouting for all he was worth. The Stribs immediately gave chase. A great commotion ensued. The Ice Maiden's medicine had done its job. The children began to shriek and shout just as you would expect if somebody charged unexpectedly through your camp in the dark.

Rag ran right across the camp, chased by the penguins. Suddenly, he stumbled and fell. Moments later, he was surrounded by what looked like every guard present. Slowly and glumly he staggered to his feet and raised his hands.

It was a signal to Loriana and she began to hum a few notes. The others watched as a twinkling light began to drift through the gloom towards the penguins. Sarah could hear the familiar faint tinkling sound and knew that the Naida had come. *That's how Oswain means to deal with the guards*, she thought.

Like a halo they descended and ringed the penguins and Rag. At once a deep sleep overcame the Stribs and one by one they bent over and fell to the ground. Even Rag himself was affected and he too swooned.

'Come on,' said Oswain. 'Now it's time for the rest of us.'

Two other rope ladders were dropped and the rest of the party quickly climbed down into the hollow. They found themselves among a lot of confused and bewildered children. Some had begun to cry, wondering what was going on in the near darkness, for the only light was the crystal above the tub of Sa.

Oswain made for it and held the glowing lamp aloft so that all could make out his features.

'Do not be afraid,' he cried. 'There is nothing to fear. We have come to rescue you.'

He was answered by a ripple of noise.

'You have been taken prisoner and drugged,' he continued. 'We have managed to give you a medicine to make you better.'

'Don't want to be better,' said one little boy. 'I'm cold and hungry. Don't like you!'

But most of the others told him to be quiet.

'How do we know you're telling the truth?' shouted an older boy.

'I am Oswain, servant of Elmesh, and ruler of the Great Forest of Alamore,' he replied.

At that a murmur ran through the children.

'Are you really the King, then?' piped up a little girl's voice.

He laughed. 'Yes, I am the King. And I have come to lead my young subjects to freedom.'

A ragged cheer went through the camp.

'We are going to lead you to a place of warmth and safety – and to food and drink,' he added.

That brought a bigger cheer.

'It will be a long journey through the night and you will be tired when you arrive, but we will do our best to keep you all safe. With me are Loriana the Ice Maiden, and my companions, Peter, Sarah and Andrew.'

A loud caw made him add, 'And Wheezer, who bravely slipped the antidote in the Sa.'

'Here is Rag, whom some of you will know,' called the Ice Maiden. She had carried him away from the sleeping penguins and revived him. Some of the children called out Rag's name.

'Is everyone ready?' Oswain cried.

'Yes,' they chorused.

'Then let's go. Follow me. Up the rope ladders.'

With a loud cry the children surged forward and the whole company began their climb out of the hollow and to freedom. Peter counted about three hundred and fifty children. It wasn't going to be easy getting them back to the safety of the jungle.

He was just wondering about this when there came a deep and ominous roll of thunder from the top of the volcano.

15

The Storm

How do you lead so many children across the open mountainside in the dark?

The more Peter thought about it, the more doubtful he felt. Rescuing them from the penguins had been remarkably easy, thanks to Wheezer and the Ice Maiden, but now that three hundred and fifty children were milling around demanding to know what happened next, it was a different matter.

For a start, none of them was dressed for a midnight hike across a frozen and treacherous landscape. Most wore only ragged animal skins over what was left of their night clothes and had bits of fur tied around their feet.

Peter wondered where the furs had come from. He also realised that the drugged drink had stopped the children from feeling the cold. Now that the effects were wearing off many of them were shivering and complaining.

'It's badly organised and thoughtless, if you ask me,' said one rather snooty child to a group of friends.

'Well, nobody's asking you!' Peter butted in.

The group gave him one of those 'who do you think you are' looks until he turned awkwardly away in the dark.

Another roll of thunder from the summit of the volcano added to his worry and unease. If only these children would do as they were told! He felt annoyed that they wouldn't line up properly. They ought to, he thought, forgetting for the moment that he wasn't very good at lining up himself when he was at school. It was a wonder nobody had slipped and fallen back into the ravine.

All in all it took a good half hour and a lot of shouting and running to and fro before they were finally lined up in a column of threes and ready for the trek across the mountains.

'At last!' Peter huffed. He was thoroughly fed up and began to wonder why they had rescued these kids in the first place. Nobody seemed very grateful. In fact, many of the older ones just treated him as one of their number, and didn't take any notice when he gave orders. He wished he had a badge or a uniform so they would know who he was.

When they did at last get moving, the Ice Maiden led the way, her shimmering form giving faint light to the shadowy column and making it look like a giant glow-worm snaking across the countryside. She had left the Naida guarding the penguins lest they should raise the alarm. Oswain brought up the rear of the party while Peter, Sarah, Andrew and Rag were spread along the column to make sure everyone was keeping together. It wasn't easy.

For all that, they made surprisingly good progress and Peter began to feel a bit better. Even the thunder from the volcano didn't seem too bad.

However, the further they advanced, the heavier the air became. Every step required more effort and it became difficult to breathe. It was the kind of night when people feel sick and headachy, and very irritable. Silence fell on the party and soon only the sound of their panting and the tramp of their feet could be heard.

Then the storm broke. It exploded with a suddenness that took their breath away. Violent jagged flashes of lightning seared across the sky, lighting up the countryside all around them. They were followed by an ear-shattering crash of thunder that whumped against the hillside like a mortar bomb. In seconds it was followed by another, and another. Oswain's face looked grim in the garish light. They were caught on the open hills in the middle of a full-blown electrical storm and he knew how dangerous and frightening that could be.

Many of the girls screamed when the lightning flashed. The boys shouted and laughed but they were desperately trying to cover up their own fear. The thunder was so loud that many had to block their ears. It was becoming more and more difficult to keep the children from panicking and running off in all directions.

'Everyone keep together,' cried Oswain above the din. 'Keep together!'

They pressed on, scrambling over obstacles, stopping for a few moments each time the storm seemed at its worst.

'Loriana was right about us upsetting whatever's in that mountain,' Andrew called to Peter.

'Just what I was thinking,' came the reply. 'I'll be glad when it's daylight and we're all back in the jungle. I'm sick to death of all this!'

Then it began to rain. At first a few heavy thunder drops fell, but then the sky opened and the rain poured down in blinding, biting, wind-driven torrents. There was nothing the company could do except stop and find what shelter they could.

There wasn't much of that in this open country and soon everyone was soaked to the skin and shivering with the cold. Worse still, as Peter quickly realised, the water was turning to ice almost as soon as it touched the ground. It would be impossible to walk on. His misgivings and annoyance began to turn to fear. He wondered if they would ever get out of this alive.

'Elmesh help us,' he muttered. 'I feel scared!'

Oswain was in conference with the Ice Maiden. 'We simply must keep going,' he said. 'Otherwise these children are going to die of exposure.'

'I agree,' she replied. 'But we must shelter until this rain eases a little. They can't see where they are treading.'

The only shelter available was on the lee-side of a pile of rocks, so that was where they huddled, waiting and praying for the rain to ease.

At length, the storm began to die down but the scene it had left behind was incredible. As far as the eye could see the landscape was a glimmering blue. Everywhere was ice. It would be like crossing an ice-rink in carpet slippers.

'This is impossible,' Sarah groaned. 'We'll never walk on that.'

'No, it's not,' Peter replied stoutly. He had suddenly, unaccountably, cheered up as the storm had passed, and now his eyes were alight with a kind of wild excitement. 'This isn't going to beat us. Don't you remember what Loriana can do? You, know, when we first met her, and Andrew and I were stuck on the mountain in the snow and she rescued us?'

'Yes, that's right.' Sarah brightened suddenly at the

memory. Trust Peter to remember, she thought. He would never forget how the Ice Maiden had saved their lives.*

'Join all the children's hands together,' Oswain ordered.

Under his direction the children formed a great long chain. The Ice Maiden took the hand of a ten-year-old named Slaf and with a cheerful 'Follow me' set off.

To their utter amazement the children found they could walk with ease on the slippery sheet ice.

'Just make sure you don't let go hands,' Oswain called from near the back.

Peter was last in line behind Oswain.

'This is great!' he cried. 'Who would have thought it would turn out like this?'

'Ah, who indeed?' Oswain smiled. 'Maybe we should have thought of this in the first place.' He gave Peter a grin and as their eyes met the boy knew that Oswain had understood just how he had been feeling earlier.

Peter began to feel better and better and soon he was singing and shouting his head off. This was a great adventure. Who's afraid of dragons and penguins and stupid orange clouds?

It was then that his renewed high spirits got the better of him. In one mad moment, as they topped a ridge, he let go of Oswain's hand and decided to slide down what looked like a gentle slope to see if he could catch up with the front of the party.

The trouble is, gentle slopes can be very deceptive, and before Peter could stop himself he found that instead of

---

* You can read all about this in *Oswain and the Mystery of the Star Stone*.

going where he wanted, he was being swept away to his left into a long gully that disappeared into the darkness.

Oswain saw what was happening at once and called to the Ice Maiden, 'Loriana, Peter's in trouble. I'm going after him. Carry on with the rest.'

Turning aside, Oswain set off down the slope in search of his young friend. He just hoped Peter hadn't slipped over a cliff at the bottom.

Sarah and Andrew were horrified at their older brother's folly.

'What an idiot!' gasped Andrew.

'You're telling me,' his sister replied. 'I do hope he's going to be all right,' she added quietly.

For a while everybody waited anxiously. At last a cheerful yell from far down below told them that things were fine.

'You carry on. We'll find our own way,' Oswain called. 'It'll take too long for us to climb back and you need to get those children to safety.'

'Just mind no one else lets go,' the Ice Maiden cautioned the children. 'Now you know what will happen!'

The rest of the journey went well and soon they were approaching the last long rise beyond which lay the safety and warmth of the jungle. Andrew was feeling decidedly hungry and was looking forward to something to eat. A whole bunch of bananas to himself, he thought.

However, their troubles were not over. The storm suddenly picked up again. The wind grew in strength and thunder began to roll. Then there was one almighty flash of lightning. It was so bright and unexpected that it temporarily blinded everyone. Children screamed and howled and fell to the ground under the onslaught of the resounding crash of thunder that followed almost at once.

As suddenly as it had come, it went, and they picked themselves up to resume their journey. However, all was not well.

'Hey, look!' exclaimed Andrew. 'What's that?'

Ahead of them over the ridge the skyline glowed bright orange. By now the ground was wet underfoot and they could walk with ease, so everyone ran to the top of the ridge.

When they reached it Andrew and Sarah's mouths dropped open with dismay. The whole jungle was on fire as far as the eye could see. The night sky burned an angry smoky red as the wind drove the flames remorselessly through the trees.

For an hour they glumly watched the retreating flames. It was the end of the jungle and their only hope of shelter, water and food.

'Now what do we do?' asked Andrew. 'We've rescued all the children and brought them to nowhere. We're in a mess!'

'Yes, and we haven't even got Oswain or Peter with us,' said Sarah. 'I do hope they're all right.'

At that moment Loriana joined them. 'We have a very determined enemy,' she said grimly. 'He certainly isn't making it easy for us.' She wrinkled her nose at the smell of the fire.

'What are we going to do, Loriana?' Andrew asked.

'I feel like giving up,' admitted Sarah.

'That you must never do,' Loriana replied. 'Hope isn't lost just because things are difficult. Have you not yet learned that lesson, Sarah?'

Her voice was kindly and Sarah smiled up at her.

'Sorry. I suppose it just feels that there's no way out. I hate this island.'

'But we're here for a purpose, and so far we've managed to set the children free. That's a start. And we haven't lost any of them yet. We've done well!' she smiled.

'And look!' cried Andrew.

He was pointing up in the sky.

'Elrilion,' breathed the Ice Maiden. 'Elrilion is risen.'

Low on the far horizon Elmesh's star hung like a perfect silver-blue sapphire. Even as they gazed at it they felt its radiance enter their hearts and fill them with an uncanny but comforting hope.

'It will be well, you'll see,' whispered the Ice Maiden.

16

Attack from the Sky

As the first glimmer of day tinged the horizon the last livid flames of the jungle fire died away.

It was a very bleak scene that the pale dawn unveiled to the company on the ridge – nothing but gaunt blackened stumps jutting from an ocean of grey ash as far as the eye could see. And the awful silence of a deserted place. No sounds of the once-living forest would be heard here for a long time to come; no rustle of wind through the trees or clattering creatures in their branches; no chirrup in the undergrowth or furtive crack of twig would break the silence. Everything was gone.

The children and their rescuers watched quietly as the eastern sky brightened. The hope which Elrilion had given faded with the rising sun – though to be sure it did not die altogether. At least they were dry and it was warmer here than on the frozen hills behind. But it was obvious to all that their hopes of food and shelter were dashed.

'Better see what we can find,' said Andrew glumly. 'At least we must look for water. None of us will last long without something to drink.'

His sister agreed and, after speaking with Loriana, they set off down the hillside, keeping to rocky outcrops and as far as possible avoiding the smouldering embers. Wheezer flew on ahead to see what he could find.

It was a miserable business walking the charred slopes. Hot ash lay everywhere and the air was acrid with smoke. Sarah and Andrew felt thoroughly gloomy.

'We really are in trouble now,' Sarah coughed. 'I just don't know how we're going to look after all those kids. And what if the penguins or . . . or that monster in the mountain attack us?'

'Maybe Oswain and Peter can come up with something,' Andrew answered.

'They should have been back by now,' his sister replied. 'I just hope they're all right. If only Peter hadn't been so stupid!'

'Yeah, but Oswain can take care of himself,' said Andrew stoutly. 'He'll even manage to look after our daft brother,' he added with a sudden laugh.

Just then Wheezer came flapping towards them.

'Down on your left,' he squawked. 'There's a spring and the water looks OK, but I've not tasted it.'

'Don't worry,' Sarah called. 'We'll take a look. You just show us the way.'

Sure enough, they found water. Andrew tasted it cautiously. It was a bit smoky but otherwise seemed all right.

'Well, that's something,' he grinned. 'All we need now is a cooked breakfast for three hundred and fifty starving children!'

Just then Wheezer cawed from overhead. 'Oh-oh, trouble!'

'What is it?' said Sarah. Her heart missed a beat and a twinge of fear shot through her.

'Up there.' He indicated the top of the volcano. Sarah looked and gasped with horror.

'Oh, boy!' Andrew gulped.

The cloud which enveloped the summit was boiling an angry orange and from its heart, spewing high into the sky, were hundreds and hundreds of dark shapes. It looked like a macabre giant firework going off. Andrew and Sarah had never seen anything like it in their lives.

Fear paralysed them. Wheezer hovered listlessly as though his wings had lost almost all their strength. He knew exactly what the dark shapes were.

'Vultures. It's them vultures again. Hundreds of 'em,' he muttered.

With an effort of will Andrew forced himself to move. He gave Sarah's arm a slap. 'We'd better get back to the others,' he urged. 'Come on, Sarah!'

His sister jolted and nodded dumbly before following him.

Back on the ridge, everyone knew something was wrong and a ripple of unease ran through the assembled children. For a moment nobody was quite sure why. Then Rag pointed to the summit of the volcano. The Ice Maiden shielded her eyes and gazed with wonder at the sight as hundreds of vultures belched from the cloud. She did not need to be told what their intentions were.

'Elmesh help us,' she whispered. 'And protect all the children.'

They watched awestruck as the huge flock of birds slowly wheeled and turned high above them, at times temporarily blocking out the sun and causing a chill shadow to fall across the crowd below. Many of the children began to scream and cry, and some started to run.

'Stay where you are!' cried Loriana urgently. 'You will be safe if you stay close to me.'

Most of the children heeded her voice and grabbed

others who wanted to run, but everyone was on the edge of panic.

'*Naida, le mera soranda!*' the Ice Maiden called. To the amazement of the children the Naida came – as swift as light – and hovered above her in a huge twinkling halo. 'Come closer and you will be all right,' she called.

At that moment, as though in response to a hidden signal, the vultures swooped. The air trembled with their terrifying screeches. Children cowered and blocked their ears; but none could keep out the message that penetrated their minds. 'Run! Run! Scatter!' It was all any of them could do to stay where they were.

The eyes of the unnatural creatures flashed red as they swooped low, bringing terror on the children. There was no mistaking their purpose. Once the children were scattered they would be easy targets to attack or to recapture for Shugob's evil plans.

The Ice Maiden knew this and with upraised arms directed the Naida to ward off the enemy. However, the Naida were few against such an enormous host and it would only be a matter of time before one or other of the children ran. Then the rest would scatter and all would be lost.

Andrew and Sarah had made it back to the main group along with Wheezer. He knew he was no match for such terrifying creatures and cowered along with the rest under the shelter of the whirling Naida.

'How long can we last out?' yelled Andrew above the din.

'I don't know,' Sarah replied. 'I just wish that Oswain was here. What's happened to them? Don't say they've been attacked as well.'

The assault was getting worse and many of the children were seriously losing their nerve. The vultures were draped over the huddled company like a huge, black writhing blanket, and the Ice Maiden's powers seemed very frail.

'I've got to do something,' Wheezer thought. 'Anything. I'm not going to die just waiting for them to get me.'

The brave old pelican made up his mind. He would fight, and die in the attempt. 'Perhaps I can draw them off a bit,' he wondered, and, against all his instincts, he took to the air and entered the fray.

'Yah, you can't catch me, silly old buzzards!' he squawked.

For a moment, the swooping vultures ignored him, so intent were they on panicking the children. The pelican continued to call. 'Elmesh is King! Elmesh is King! Shugob is rubbish!'

That did it. The angry, almost mindless vultures, unable to refuse the taunt, turned on him like a gigantic storm cloud and attacked. Wheezer streaked away as fast as his wings could carry him. It wasn't much to offer, but he knew he had to do it. In a few moments he would be dead, but he wouldn't die a coward – and maybe it would help his friends just enough.

The nearest vulture was almost upon him as he offered his simple pelican soul to Elmesh. 'I did what I could, sir,' he muttered. 'Hope I did right. I'm ready to meet you, but please help my friends.'

At that moment, there came the most heart-stopping, chilling screech he had ever heard. He felt as if he was being pierced by a thousand needles of ice, colder,

sharper than anything he could ever have imagined.
Again the scream echoed across the frozen hills and they
seemed to shiver at the sound.

The vultures, distracted by the noise, at once called off
their attack and wheeled in confusion. Wheezer swooped
round to confront the new menace.

What a sight greeted his eyes! Streaking out of the sun,
wings glinting white in the morning light, came a bird the
size and splendour of which he had never seen before in
his life – and not one but seemingly hundreds followed
him. Wheezer's heart leapt. Something told him they
were good. Terrifyingly good!

'He's sent in the air force. Elmesh has sent in the whole
blooming air force!' the pelican gasped. 'Well, frazzle me
feathers!'

On the ground the Ice Maiden whirled at the sound and
her face broke into a beaming smile. Most of the children
hadn't realised what was happening and lay screaming
and sobbing on the ground thinking this must be some
new horror. But Andrew and Sarah knew better.

'It's Arca!' cried Sarah. 'He's come. Andrew, he's come!
We're going to be saved.' At once she burst into tears.

Andrew looked up and blinked. He felt a lump in his
throat and swallowed hard.

'Arca,' he repeated. 'Elmesh has heard us.'

In seconds, a host of white eagles fell upon the vultures.
Mercilessly and ruthlessly they attacked the foul carrion,
drowning their cries with their own victorious screeches.
Even those vultures that sought refuge in the summit of
the volcano found their path cut off. None of this devilish
brood was to be spared.

The children began to realise that these terrifying eagles

were on their side as they heard Andrew and Sarah cheering for all they were worth. Some of the older ones rose to their feet.

'Go on, get them!' shouted Andrew. 'Knock 'em for six!'

'Hurray for Arca!' Sarah cried. 'Go for them! Tear them apart!'

Soon all the children were on their feet, many clutching one another and cheering their heads off as they saw their enemies overpowered and destroyed.

Loriana stood in silent thankful wonder, her arms raised in gratitude. They were saved.

The battle didn't last long, and soon not a vulture was to be seen. Then one by one, the white eagles settled on the hillside, covering it like newly fallen snow ruffled in a light breeze. The Ice Maiden hastened to meet their magnificent leader.

It was too far away for anyone to hear what they said but at last she turned towards them and waved. 'Arca!' she cried triumphantly.

'Arca! Arca!' they chanted in response.

'Three cheers for Arca,' cried Andrew above the din. 'Hip, hip hurray!'

'Hurray!' the children responded, and again, and again.

Sarah turned to her brother, her eyes full of excitement. 'You know, it's just like the tide is turning,' she said. 'At last we're fighting back. I'm so glad Arca's come. Isn't it amazing?'

So it was, for the Ice Maiden returned to tell them that their deliverer had come with the greatest force possible and even more were on their way from all parts of the world. Sarah wondered why so many were needed, but said nothing.

During the next hour they cleared a path to the water brook. Then, to Andrew's immense delight, the eagles flew away and returned with all sorts of food for the children.

'But I wish I knew where Peter and Oswain had got to,' said Sarah as she munched an apple.

'They're on to something, I reckon,' Andrew replied. 'I just wonder what it is.'

17

Oswain and Peter Strike Back

'I'm sorry,' Peter muttered sheepishly as Oswain slithered down to join him at the bottom of the valley. He was relieved that the darkness hid his face, because he knew he looked shaken and embarrassed.

'Hm, it was a rather foolish notion,' puffed the King as he reached him. 'Still, no matter. It seems that you are unhurt and that is the main thing.'

Oswain gazed back up the shadowy-blue slope. It was dimly lit by the starlight and he could only just make out the ridge from which they had slid. The company was completely out of sight.

'There's no way we are going to climb that,' he observed. 'And I don't want Loriana to waste time fetching us and leaving the children alone. They would panic without her, I fear.'

He called to the main party to tell them that he and Peter would find their own way back and join the rest in the jungle.

'If we stay on the lower ground, with care we should manage. But no more sliding down slopes, eh?' he grinned.

Peter felt better now that he knew Oswain wasn't angry with him. As they began their trek through the darkness it struck him that, with friends, apologies and forgiveness did not need many words; you just had to really mean it. He was glad Oswain was his friend.

Although they both had good balance, the ground was uneven and they made slow progress on the treacherous ice. *At this rate, it'll be daybreak before we get back*, Peter thought.

Suddenly, Oswain motioned him to stop. It was still very dark but the ice gleamed cold under the stars and their eyes had adjusted to see a fair way. He urged Peter down to a crouching position and pointed.

'What is it?' Peter whispered.

'On the hillside,' hissed Oswain. 'Look, there is somebody or something watching.'

Peter saw what he meant. A large dark figure stood out like a sentinel.

'What do you think?' Peter asked.

'Could be a guard,' Oswain replied. 'In which case he must be guarding something, and that may be of interest to us.'

'I'm game,' Peter answered, guessing what was on Oswain's mind. 'Let's take a look.'

Keeping low, the two companions worked around and up the hillside until they were on a level with the sentinel. Fortunately, the rock was fairly jumbled just here and they could move safely without being spotted.

Soon they were close enough to get a better view.

'Ah,' breathed Oswain.

'He hasn't moved,' Peter hissed.

'No, and nor will he,' Oswain answered. 'It's a very interesting statue.' He patted Peter on the shoulder. 'Hm, your slide may have turned out all right after all! Let's take a closer look.'

The feeling of lightness which Oswain's words gave Peter was quickly quenched as they approached the squat figure. Seldom had he felt such a sense of heaviness and despair, nor such uncanny power, as though a ghost inhabited the statue. His hair bristled on the nape of his neck and he found himself trembling uncontrollably.

Oswain had none of those fears, or if he did he never showed them.

'Behold, the Image of Shugob!' he said quietly as they reached the statue.

Peter saw that it glowed a faint orange.

'Shugob! Is this Shugob?' Peter gulped. 'Is this the one who is controlling the penguins?'

'If you mean only this Image, no. If you mean the real power at work through this wretched idol, then yes,' Oswain answered grimly. 'Shugob the Almighty. A loathsome lie! A deceiver! And a hater of children.'

Peter could feel Oswain's anger even in the dark. He felt suddenly a very small boy in the presence of great powers, for he realised that this was a real idol and that Oswain was a real king.

'Wh . . . what are we going to do?' he stammered.

Oswain turned, his eyes blazing in the dim light. 'There is only one thing to do with such idols and false gods, and that is to destroy them before they destroy others.'

Peter recalled hearing that if things were works of art, they shouldn't be destroyed, whatever they stood for – and it got all mixed up in his mind with a fear of touching this Image. He had never before met a living idol and realised that most of the people who talked about art and idols hadn't either.

'Idols have power only while people worship them,'

Oswain said, sensing the boy's uncertainty. 'But when the times are ripe, some idols revive their old power and draw new worshippers. So it is with Shugob.'

'How on earth did it get here? On this island, I mean.'

'It began in the days when my parents were much younger and before they had met,' Oswain answered. 'Shugob broke into Caris Meriac from another realm, as we told you earlier. He soon had devoted followers – fear-ridden people who bowed to hooded priests and in ignorance offered their children as sacrifices to what they called the sky god. They thought this was the way to make the world a happier place!' He grimaced.

'That . . . that's just so stupid!' said Peter.

'Sure it is, but people are more easily deceived than they like to think,' Oswain replied. 'Anyway, as you now know, my father drove Shugob from Caris Meriac and back to his own realm; but his followers fled.'

'They came here. To Aethius?'

'Indeed, and we heard that they built an idol to continue worshipping Shugob. We heard, too, about a young dragon who feasted on the sacrificed children.'

'Tergan!'

'The very same.'

'Ugh! And we were so close to him,' Peter said with a shudder. 'He's no baby now, either.'

'The last we heard was that the island had sunk,' Oswain continued. 'That was the end of it as far as we were concerned. The idol, the dragon, the followers, all drowned.' He frowned. 'No one expected the lost island to rise again, let alone everything else that has happened. We should have been more watchful.'

'What are we going to do?' Peter asked. He looked

dubiously at the idol and then back to Oswain. The idol seemed to flicker in the darkness and the air smelt bad.

'Destroy it, of course,' Oswain replied.

Peter swallowed his fears and doubts and nodded. 'All right,' he gulped. 'How are we, I mean you, going to get rid of it?'

Oswain eyed Peter keenly. 'You suggest a way,' he answered.

'Well, how about pushing it down the mountainside?' Peter ventured.

Oswain agreed. 'Fine. We'll push together.'

So, they got behind the Image and began to push. Peter wasn't sure if it was his imagination, but he could feel his hands tingling as he touched the stone. Even next to Oswain he was having to fight to stop himself running away from the Image.

In spite of their combined weight and determination, the figure refused to budge. Oswain motioned Peter off and drew his sword. The boy watched wide-eyed as Oswain touched the base of the idol with the glowing tip. He heard Oswain call upon Elmesh.

At that moment lightning flashed across the sky. It was followed by a deafening crash of thunder.

Then, to Peter's amazement, the idol began to glow. But not the orange he expected. A blue light glimmered where Oswain's sword was touching the stone. It spread across the idol, then seemed to set it ablaze from within. Suddenly, with a loud cracking sound the Image began to craze all over.

Moments later the idol shattered, falling like a rush of broken ice cubes down the hillside. Then Peter heard a doleful sigh pass into the night. At once the atmosphere lightened, as though some awful threat, like a panther stalking in the undergrowth, had been removed. His fears dissolved and he felt happy again.

Oswain sheathed his sword.

'There, it is done, and not before time,' he said. 'Well done, Peter.'

'But I didn't do it, you did,' the boy replied meekly.

'Yes, but I knew from the beginning that I could. You, against your doubts and fears, chose to attempt it even though you did not know if you had the power. Yours is the real victory tonight.'

Peter wasn't sure if he understood, but nodded anyway. It sounded important and maybe one day it would make sense to him. He smiled. 'You know, I feel really happy. It's just so right that we broke it. I felt scared but now it seems, well, clean around here, and safe.'

Oswain nodded thoughtfully. 'Cleaner and safer. Yes. Yes, you are right, Peter. Though there is still much to be done,' he added.

With lighter steps they began their journey once more; but they had hardly gone any distance when they stumbled across an opening in the hillside.

'Another tunnel!' cried Peter.

Oswain urged him to speak softly.

'Yes, and so near to the Image,' he murmured. 'I wonder . . .'

He seemed to make up his mind. 'Come on, Peter,' he said. 'I think it's time we did something about that key which Sarah was forced to make – and I have a feeling we shall find the answer somewhere in here.'

'I'm coming,' said Peter. He knew how his sister felt about the key and he wanted to help destroy it before it could do the damage it was designed for.

They crept into the tunnel. It was very long and as they edged through the darkness, Peter began to wonder where it led. He feared that one of them might take a fatal step and fall into an unseen mine shaft or pit.

At length there was a faint glow ahead and, a few minutes later, they saw that they had passed right through the mountain and were emerging into the penguins' lair. The light came from one of the crystals set in the wall. Oswain cautioned Peter to go very slowly.

To their left was an open cubicle. They crept to the entrance and, lying on his stomach, Oswain took a look round. He edged back and Peter took his place. 'It's Yarx!' he mouthed.

Oswain nodded and slowly drew his sword. The next moment he whirled through the doorway and had the point at the chief Strat's throat before Yarx could so much as move a muscle to raise the alarm.

'Stay where you are,' ordered Oswain. He pressed the point home meaningfully. 'Don't move, or I shall use this,' he threatened. 'Just one sound will be enough.'

The penguin remained motionless and Peter could see that his eyes were full of anger.

'What do you want?' he croaked.

'The key,' Oswain snapped. 'You will give me the key.'

At this the penguin flinched.

'I cannot do that,' he answered. 'It belongs to the Lord whom I serve. I will only use it to fulfil the Great Purpose.'

'The Great Purpose is evil and we shall not allow it,' Oswain replied curtly. 'Now, take us to the key.' He prodded the penguin in the throat. 'And no tricks.'

'The Great Purpose is everything,' Yarx snapped. 'It

must come to pass. It is decreed by the gods and the planets. You cannot thwart it.'

'I am Oswain, servant of Elmesh. He did not order this so-called Great Purpose. You are deluded, Yarx. Now where is the key?'

'It's all right, Oswain,' Peter called. 'I think I've found something. Over here.'

Yarx growled angrily when he saw what Peter had discovered. Oswain gave it a sidelong glance. On a shelf of ice stood a wire pyramid in the centre of which hovered an orange crystal. He had no doubt that this was the key that Sarah had made.

'Pick it up, Yarx,' he ordered, emphasising his words with the point of his sword.

The penguin glowered but reluctantly did as he was commanded.

'Now what?' Peter asked.

'Now we take it from here and find a way of destroying it,' Oswain smiled. 'It must, as with all such objects, be unmade.'

'It cannot be,' protested Yarx again. 'Peace and prosperity depend on it.'

'All your interest is in power,' snapped Oswain. 'You have strayed from your rightful path in search of it. You know nothing of what you are really dealing with. If you had, you would never have embarked on such a foolish scheme.'

'It is you who know nothing,' cawed the penguin defiantly. 'Your god is an old superstition. The future belongs to us. To Shugob and Tergan – and to the Prophetess, Kinera. Together we will rule the world in peace and prosperity.'

'This is all a waste of time,' interrupted Peter. 'Come on, Oswain. Let's get going.'

'I agree,' said Oswain. 'Now let's see how that old dragon likes a taste of this key being dropped into his bed!'

'Is that where we're going?' gasped Peter openmouthed. 'Into Tergan's lair?'

'That's right,' Oswain smiled grimly. 'And Yarx is going to lead us there.'

'No, no!' screeched the penguin. 'I cannot take the heat. I will perish. You must not make me.'

'But you want to unite ice and fire,' insisted Oswain. 'You are a creature of ice and Tergan of the fire. It will be an interesting meeting. Now move!'

With that he urged the penguin forward at swordpoint.

Peter followed anxiously. He had never seen Oswain so roused. And Tergan was stirring. He wondered how on earth they were going to get into the dragon's cave – let alone get out again alive.

18

What Andrew and Sarah Decided

'Keep close, Peter,' Oswain ordered.

They were hurrying along one of the main tunnels inside the penguins' headquarters, and Oswain was driving the waddling chief Strat hard with the tip of his sword. It was, naturally, impossible to do this in secret and in a very short time the news of Yarx's capture had spread throughout the Strib encampment. A large company of penguins armed with ice spears had gathered and now followed at a watchful distance. Others lining the route stood aside as their leader passed through. Peter could feel the hostility in the air.

'Make one move and your leader dies!' Oswain warned. His voice was grim and his eye as keen as the sharp steel of his sword. Nobody dared to challenge him.

They seemed to be walking for a very long time and Peter began to wonder whether Yarx wasn't just leading them in circles. He had no idea of his bearings and although every so often an entrance or corner appeared vaguely familiar, as soon as they reached it he found there was nothing to mark it out from all the rest. Oswain was having the same thoughts.

'That will do Yarx,' he ordered. 'Stop! You seem to have lost your way on your own territory. How surprising! Perhaps then, there is no point in keeping you alive. Maybe we should find some other, more reliable guide.' He pressed the tip of his sword hard against the penguin's neck and for a moment Peter thought that Oswain might kill him.

Yarx was unmoved. 'We are almost at the entrance to Tergan's lair,' he replied gruffly without turning round. 'It is along this passage and to the left.'

'Very well,' Oswain answered curtly. 'But no tricks.'

Sure enough, up ahead was a turning off to the left. In less than a minute they had drawn level with it.

That was when things went wrong.

The penguin made the turn with a sudden burst of speed – so fast that Oswain and Peter were for a moment caught off guard. Turning the corner themselves, they at once hit a steep and slippery slope and before either could stop themselves they were tumbling and slithering head-long into a waiting icy pit.

It was all over in seconds. Glumly the two companions untangled themselves and looked up. There stood Yarx, perched on a narrow ledge above the trap, his bright eyes gleaming with satisfaction. He laughed mockingly and held out the key with a sneer of triumph. There was nothing either of them could do about it.

'You are a fool, Oswain, and the brat with you. Nothing can stop us; not you, nor your Elmesh. Shugob is supreme. One more sunrise and he will come in power and glory! The Great Purpose begins!'

With that the chief Strat threw a small capsule into the pit. It belched orange smoke as it fell. The last thing Oswain and Peter remembered was his arrogant face disappearing behind the fumes. Then everything went dark as they slumped unconscious to the floor.

* * *

Sarah and Andrew were growing restless.

They were seated together on a rock overlooking the sea. Nothing much was happening and most of the children were simply sitting in groups chatting in the mild sunshine; some were asleep on the ground. Arca and the great host of eagles remained settled at a distance on the mountainside and did not seem inclined to invite company. Only the Ice Maiden had been allowed to speak with Arca, and Sarah felt more than a little put out over this.

'I'm worried about Peter and Oswain,' she said, breaking the silence abruptly. 'They should have been back by now.'

Andrew nodded. 'Me too. I'd like to know what's going on. Why aren't Loriana and Arca talking to us, anyway? It's almost as though they were treating us just like the rest of the kids.' He gave a disdainful sniff. 'After all, we are supposed to be, well, their friends, aren't we?'

Sarah nodded, then kicked a pebble aimlessly. 'I suppose there's a reason for it. Though I wish they'd tell us what. I mean, something incredible is going to happen soon, what with the dragon and Shugob and all that. I guess it's just too important for the likes of us.'

Andrew glanced at his sister. She looked as glum as he felt.

Just then they spotted the Ice Maiden approaching them. They rose expectantly. She greeted them with a smile but Sarah could see she was worried.

'There is much to be done and quickly,' she said. 'I have decided with Arca that the children should be removed to safety as soon as possible. He and the other eagles will transport you all to another island several miles from here and then they will take everyone to their own homes later on.'

'What, us as well? Have we got to go with them?' cried Andrew with dismay.

She nodded with a grave smile. 'I'm sorry, but it's for the best. It is simply too dangerous here.'

The children tried to protest but she held up her hand. 'I'm sorry,' was all she would say.

'But what about Peter and Oswain? Where are they?' Sarah insisted. She could feel her face growing red.

'That I do not know at present,' the Ice Maiden replied. 'Like you, I wait for some news.' She looked at them solemnly for a few moments and then turned abruptly to begin organising the children for their journey.

Sarah was almost in tears and was also very angry. 'Why can't we stay? If Oswain and Peter are in danger, we might as well be in it with them. I feel we're deserting them just when they need us most.'

Andrew nodded and put his arm round his sister's shoulder. For a long time neither said a word. Then they turned and looked each other straight in the eye. With nothing spoken, both nodded. Brother and sister understood one another. Whatever happened to the rest of the children, they would be staying.

Their chance came more easily than they expected. That afternoon, Loriana led the company of children in a column up the mountainside to where the eagles perched waiting. The shattered rock and boulder-strewn path offered many places to hide and it took only a moment for Andrew and Sarah to slip off unnoticed into a gully between two tall stones.

'I do hope we're doing the right thing,' Sarah whispered as the file of children passed into the distance.

'Of course we are,' Andrew answered. 'I don't really

think Loriana wanted to get rid of us. It's just that she's worried about Oswain and Peter and wants to get everyone she can to safety.' Andrew wasn't sure whether that was really the case or whether he just hoped it was so that he would feel all right about disobeying her wishes.

Sarah agreed. 'We've got to find them. I just know they're in trouble somewhere and I'm sure it's inside that hateful mountain.'

It wasn't long before they could hear a loud swishing of wings and the high-pitched cries of excited children as the eagles bore them away. Each child was seated astride an eagle's back. Sarah remembered with envy her own rides on Arca's broad shoulders and knew how marvellous they must be feeling. For a moment she wished she was with them.

There were many more eagles than were needed to take the children to safety but for some reason all of them left the island together. Soon the mountainside was quite bare. The whole operation had taken no more than half an hour.

Andrew and Sarah watched the solitary figure of the Ice Maiden striding back down the mountainside. Just once she glanced sharply behind her as if aware of something. Sarah wanted to run after her to say they were still here. She suddenly felt lonely, and afraid.

Andrew nudged her. 'Time to start climbing,' he said.

Neither knew what dangers might be awaiting them inside the orange cloud that covered the summit. They had no idea how they were going to reach Oswain and Peter either. But it didn't matter. They had to try – even though it might prove to be the last thing they ever did.

Sarah and Andrew may have been expecting monsters

or some kind of violent attack, but the enemy had other, more subtle, ways of resisting them. For the first half-hour they climbed easily, but then every step became an immense effort, every movement slow, reluctant and wearisome. With each passing minute their sense of doom grew. It was like climbing into fear itself.

The afternoon wore on and the sun began to sink. The deep orange glow of the cloud became more livid than ever. They scarcely dared look at it.

'I . . . I don't think I can go on,' Sarah gasped. 'Andrew, help me, please!'

She slumped limply against a rock. Andrew struggled towards her. 'I know how you feel,' he panted. 'But we've got to do it, Sis. For Pete and Oswain's sake, we've got to do it!'

He stared earnestly at her until her eyes met his. She nodded bleakly.

Darkness fell and still they toiled up that awful mountainside. By now they had no idea how far they had come or how far it was to the summit. All they could manage was to force one leg in front of the other. Even to do this was so painful that they had to bite their lips with every step.

Entering the cloud itself was terrifying. The first orange wisps felt like the brushing of loathsome giant cobwebs. Sarah shivered and screamed and Andrew cried out in alarm. They huddled close and stood trembling as the misty webs reached out and stroked at their bodies, clinging to their legs, encircling their necks and smothering their faces. The sense of deep, knowing evil was almost overwhelming.

All was now dark save for the faint sheen of orange up

above them. Their skin crawling, the two children pressed on into the cloud. There was no sound except for the gasping of their lungs as they staggered upwards. All the while the orange glow grew brighter and more sinister.

The weight of the atmosphere pressed in on them and although the ground was still frozen, the air felt hot and sultry. Before long they were reduced to crawling on their hands and knees, dragging their perspiring bodies towards the summit, fighting despair with every breath.

It's hell! We're crawling upwards into some kind of hell, thought Sarah. *This is mad. But we've got to go on, and on, and on . . . maybe for ever!*

How long it lasted, how deep into the night, they could not say. The ground still rose and though at times it levelled off it was only to mock them with another false ridge. But now they were crawling upwards on their bellies, unable to stand at all.

'Too much. It's too much,' Andrew said. 'Sarah, we'll never make it.'

They lay exhausted on the ground and gazed hopelessly into each other's drawn, sweat-streaked faces. Sarah groaned out loud.

'Andrew, don't you realise? She knew. Loriana knew we'd stayed behind! I can tell. Why didn't she stop us? We've got in such a mess.'

Andrew gulped and grasped his sister's hand.

Just at that moment they heard a voice. 'My, you have done well, haven't you? Welcome to my world, Sarah, and Andrew.'

Hearts pounding fit to burst, they looked up. There in the swirling orange mist stood a woman cloaked in russet fur, and in her hand she held a lyre.

19
Kinera's World

Sarah and Andrew could scarcely believe their eyes. The woman stood within a kaleidoscope of living images that hovered in the swirling orange fog. In some, guns blazed from tall bleak battlements while soldiers fought and died on the ground below. Aeroplanes, helicopters, and flying machines that they did not recognise, fired rockets and dropped bombs whose explosions wrecked cities and countryside alike. In others, tall white ships sailed on tropical waters and the smoke of cannon-fire rose from their bulwarks as they attacked one another. In one, a tall tower stood on a silent beach in sinister stillness as though it hid terrible secrets. A grubby stone city of the kind that Andrew and Sarah might recognise in their own world, filled another. It lay dark and forbidding and serpents slithered among its tangled streets and courtyards. One scene showed nothing but a deep and crumbling chasm down which endless crowds passed mournfully to the darkness beneath.

There was Elmar, a city of white stone and fair fountains, but now frozen in ice where wolves and wild bears roamed the parks, and shadows flitted among the towers.

'Who are you?' Sarah gasped. 'And how do you know our names?'

The woman gave a twisted smile. 'I am known by other names in other worlds, but you may call me Kinera,' she replied. 'As for your names, well, let us just say that I have known of you in the past.' The smile faded. 'Not, I may add, that it was for me a pleasant past.'

'I . . . I mean . . . we've never met you before,' Andrew stuttered.

'Indeed, no. But you played a part in causing me much pain,' the woman replied. Although her tone was smooth, menace lay behind her words and it cast a chill of fear on the two exhausted children. 'I flit between many worlds and some are, as you see, full of violence. Here in Caris Meriac I had hoped I might rest, but it has, twice, treated me badly.'

'Why did you come here, then?' asked Andrew. 'Why come back to a place that you don't like?'

'I can't think what we might have done to harm you,' said Sarah. 'I mean, Andrew's right. We've never even seen you before.' She hesitated. 'At least, I don't think so.'

'Perhaps you are not quite sure, Sarah,' the woman suggested. 'Be that as it may, it will do little harm for me to tell you something of the tale and it will while away the last hours before the dawn of the new world. But I should warn you,' she added. 'I am known by some as the Prophetess, and by others as the Liar, so you may not be sure of what I tell you, but then again, how will you be sure that those who call me a liar are not themselves liars? In my world all good people may be bad, and all bad people good.'

Exhausted as they were by their climb, Sarah and Andrew did not know what to say, so all they could do was lay slumped on the frozen ground while the woman sat herself with dignity on a nearby rock.

'I will answer your question, young man,' she began, and with her hand she pushed back the hair from her brow.

'Long ago, when I was very young, I had a son. The father's name was Thello, but we were parted before the child was born and they never met. A great and glorious war made it impossible, you see. All the world's portals were torn and I searched many realms to find him, but without success. So I sought a guide to help me, a great master named Malik.'

'Why didn't you ask Elmesh?' Sarah ventured. She was racking her brains to think where she had heard the name Malik before.

The woman laughed. 'Elmesh? Elmesh died in the great war. Did you not know that?'

Sarah's unease grew even more intense. 'That's impossible,' she said. 'How can Elmesh die?'

'The woman's eyes narrowed. 'I was there,' she said. 'I saw him die.'

'I don't believe you. You're lying!'

The woman shrugged with indifference. 'Malik, the great Malik, took charge of my son's upbringing and taught him wisdom and, in the course of time, found him a place in Caris Meriac.' She frowned. 'I came in all innocence to visit my son. I visited the capital of the west as an envoy of peace and culture – and what happened? I will tell you. I was driven out and my reputation smeared. I was insulted!' Her face contorted and the children could see the rage just below the surface.

'W . . . what was the name of your son?' Andrew stammered.

'His name was Zarbid!'

Sarah gasped loudly at the news.

'Yes,' said the woman, nodding. 'Zarbid, my son, whom you plotted to kill – and you succeeded. Curses on you and all your kind!'

Sarah and Andrew were nonplussed. Zarbid had been the evil force behind Surin of Traun, the ruler of Kraan. It was Zarbid who had planned to seize the throne for himself and who had launched the attack on Oswain's kingdom. Zarbid had tried to destroy the Ice Maiden. And now, here they were, confronted by his mother.

'I watched it all from the red star,' she sneered, seeing their discomfort. 'I do not know how you won and nor could I reach him, but I saw . . . and I vowed revenge.'

'Is that why you've come back?' Andrew asked, finding his voice at last.

'Come back? Yes. But you should not fear me. I am only the agent of someone else, someone you really should fear. Even I would not trust him – but I welcome him.'

'You mean Shugob, don't you?' said Sarah, as the penny dropped. 'You're the one helping Shugob. I . . . I bet it's you that's made the penguins turn evil and . . . and caught all those children.'

'Clever little madam, aren't we?' the woman sneered. 'Oh, yes, and don't look so smug. I know you've managed to rescue those children. It doesn't matter. When Shugob comes he will have them, and countless more – and he can start on you two, can't he? I will enjoy that.'

'It won't work,' tried Andrew.

'What won't work, tell me? It already has. Everything is in place and I will give the signal at dawn.' She laughed. 'It is even better than I had hoped. All of you are on this island, you who destroyed my son. Well, I shall see you all ruined, and all the children everywhere!'

'You're mad, that's what you are!' exclaimed Sarah.

'Then you are at the mercy of a mad woman, in the dark, on top of a frozen mountain on the eve of your doom,' she replied with a laugh. Her face suddenly relaxed and she took her lyre in her hands. 'And now, I shall play you a little music,' she said.

While they had been talking both Sarah and Andrew had felt their strength returning. Andrew reached across and gave Sarah's hand a squeeze. She flashed him a look in return and, the moment Kinera began to play, they leapt to their feet and began to run.

'Try to get back to Loriana,' Andrew gasped. 'It's our only chance.'

It was easier said than done. All around them was jumbled and broken rock and the only light was the ghostly orange glow from the cloud. Neither knew which way to turn and they just made for what looked like the easiest route.

'Don't listen to the music,' Sarah cried, as they began their rapid descent.

All at once they heard a snarling sound behind them. Andrew glanced over his shoulder and got the shock of his life. Leaping down on him was a large and ferocious-looking weasel. He cried out and Sarah turned to see what had happened and without waiting rushed to help her brother. Somehow she grabbed the creature by its fur and flung it with all her might. With a squeal it vanished into the darkness.

'Come on!' she gasped.

They scrambled down the mountainside with even more urgency, conscious now that they were being pursued by a wild animal that could see better than they in the dark and that could follow their scent. Slithering and sliding on the icy rocks, they risked life and limb to escape to safety.

'Is it still following us?' Andrew panted when they slowed to cross a tricky piece of rock.

'Dunno. Don't want to wait and find out,' Sarah answered.

'Why is that, my dear?' said a woman's voice.

They whirled round at the sound and there she was again, standing before them and plucking at her lyre.

'Run for it!' Andrew cried.

Once again they heard the snarl of a weasel and this time Sarah saw enough to realise that the woman could change shape. Not that it helped, for the weasel snaked around the rocks faster than the children and they realised that there was no way they could outrun it.

Sure enough, after another helter-skelter sprint on their part, Kinera appeared before them once again and began to play. Then Sarah had an idea.

Repeating to herself, *Elmesh is alive, Elmesh is alive*, she walked towards the woman as though entranced by the music. Then, at the last moment she grabbed the lyre and tore it from the woman's hands, crying out at the same time, 'Run, Andrew! Run!'

The effect was instant; the woman changed into her weasel form before Sarah's eyes. Wasting no time, she pounced on it and rammed the lyre over its head, trapping its body and forelegs between the strings while it howled and spat at her.

'Andrew, help,' she cried. 'We need something to tie her down.'

Andrew rushed to her aid at the same time rummaging in his pockets. 'I've got this,' he said, and he pulled out a length of vine. 'I was keeping it as a souvenir from when I fell off the cliff,' he explained.

'Fantastic. Now help me tie her down,' Sarah gasped as she wrestled with the weasel.

Between them they managed to attach the animal's legs to the lyre so that it couldn't get free and, hopefully, if it changed back to the woman, would break the lyre in the process.

'I hate doing that,' said Sarah, 'but it's her or us and we've just got to get away.'

'Can't be helped,' said Andrew. 'If we'd gone on running like that we would have either fallen or broken our legs, or something.'

'Let's just hope it holds,' Sarah replied, and with that they began the next part of their descent to what they hoped was safety.

They made slow work in the darkness and seemed to be nowhere near coming out of the ice and onto warmer ground. Hour after hour went by and they were both dizzy with exhaustion.

'You know what?' said Andrew. 'I think we've come down the wrong side of the mountain. We're on the inside of the volcano, not the outside. That's why we're still in the ice. We're nowhere near Loriana.'

Sarah was close to tears. What her brother said made sense and she knew it. 'I can't go on. Got to sleep,' she sighed. 'We'll never climb back up there.'

Andrew agreed and, knowing they were completely exhausted, they huddled together, hoped for the best, and fell fast asleep. Meanwhile, up above them a furious Kinera was piecing together a broken lyre, but in spite of her rage, her mind was no longer on Andrew and Sarah. She had a far bigger prize in mind, and soon it would be dawn.

20

Lord Yarx Makes his Move

'Oh, my head! Eugh! Where am I?'

Peter opened his eyes, then shut them again quickly. The light was too bright, too painful. When he tried again a few moments later it was easier; a fuzzy, unfocused face leaned over him, shutting out the harsh glare above.

At first, he couldn't recognise the face, but the voice was familiar. It was Oswain's. He smiled with relief. They were both still alive.

'Come on, up you sit,' Oswain urged. 'You'll soon feel better.'

Assisted by Oswain's strong arms, Peter obeyed and felt his head clear as he sat upright. He looked around him. Everything was lit with a ghastly orange brightness.

'Wh . . . where are we?' he asked.

'Imprisoned in one of their pyramids, I'm afraid.' Oswain grimaced. 'See for yourself.'

Sure enough they were surrounded on all four sides by transparent but unbreakable crystalline walls. Peter got up and kicked against one hopelessly. It didn't even bend.

'So now what?' he said. 'Hey, can't you use your sword . . .?'

Oswain opened his hands and shrugged.

'How stupid!' Peter grinned wryly. 'I should have known they wouldn't let you keep it!'

'By the look of things we are inside the crater,' Oswain

175

explained. 'Over there are the igloos, and there in front of us is another pyramid.'

'I bet that's where they've got the South Pole,' said Peter.

The other pyramid was no more than a hundred metres away across a flat stretch of ice. It glowed dully in the orange light.

'What are we going to do, Oswain?' he asked. 'I mean, how are we going to stop them? We need a miracle.'

'I agree,' he answered. 'But miracles do not always come to order.'

'But something's got to happen,' Peter insisted. 'If Yarx is telling the truth the key is going to be used today.'

They were just pondering what this would mean, especially for all the children, when suddenly there was a tapping noise behind them. Both whirled round to see what was causing it.

'Andrew!' gasped Oswain in amazement. 'And Sarah!'

They rushed to the wall of the pyramid where outside the two children were gesturing wildly. Their voices sounded a bit muffled but Oswain and Peter could hear them asking what they should do to get them out.

'Find my sword, if you can?' Oswain suggested. 'Or is Loriana with you?'

They shook their heads.

'Strange that they should be alone in such a dangerous place,' Oswain said, half to himself and half to Peter. 'Even so, there is now at least some hope of escape. It looks as though you may have your miracle after all, Peter!'

However, any chance of doing something right away was brought to an end by the sound of great chords of music that echoed across the crater. Andrew and Sarah hurriedly ducked behind a nearby outcrop, while Peter and Oswain rushed to the other side of their prison to see what was going on.

As if on cue, marching out from the largest of the igloos came what looked like the full company of Stribs. All armed with spears and in tight formation, the penguins waddled across the ice towards the pyramids. As they did so, Oswain and Peter could faintly hear them chanting.

> 'We are one together
> We are one with Shugob . . .'

'You'd think they were all brainwashed,' observed Peter.

Oswain looked a little puzzled at the term but said, 'If you mean they have lost the power to think for themselves, then I am sure you are correct.'

'Hey, you don't think they're coming to kill us, do you?' exclaimed Peter, suddenly feeling afraid.

'We'll see,' Oswain replied.

They didn't have long to wait. The Stribs formed themselves into two long ranks facing one another across a broad space between the two pyramids. Peter could see where the Great Channel finished at the foot of the other pyramid. He knew that it led across the icy plain straight into Tergan's lair, and he guessed that was where the key would slide once it was released. He could only dimly imagine what would happen after that.

Then came the leaders, Lord Yarx accompanied by Senators Raaz and Kig. Yarx carried the key. Raaz held Oswain's sword. With great pomp and ceremony, they advanced to where Oswain and Peter stood watching.

Yarx stepped forward. He bowed mockingly to Oswain and laughed.

'I have saved you for this moment,' he crowed. 'I want you to witness the powerlessness of your Elmesh and the might of Shugob. It will be the last thing that you will ever see. Farewell, foolish worshippers of Elmesh!'

With that the three Strats turned and slowly walked between the ranks of Stribs towards the great pyramid. All Oswain could do was strike the walls of his prison in frustration.

Standing about twenty paces from the other pyramid, Lord Yarx raised aloft the wire frame in which the glowing key was suspended.

'The time has come!' he declared triumphantly. 'Now is the hour of fulfilment for all our labours. Shugob shall descend. Tergan shall rise. And we will reign with them over all Caris Meriac. All creatures will submit. All children will serve the new age which is dawning. Let the pyramid be opened, by the might of Shugob!'

At his words, the key flashed and sparkled and the great crystal structure before him seemed to melt away. The South Pole was revealed in all its glory.

Oswain and Peter had never seen anything like it. The pole, gleaming and glistening like a sceptre of living light, was topped with a huge star of sparkling icicles that radiated in all directions. It was alive, that was all you could say about it. Every colour of the rainbow flashed and burned within its crystalline depths. A deep drone filled the air and behind that, music – eerie, awesome music, like stars singing, Peter thought. In the South Pole there dwelt an ancient, timeless power which could as easily create life as destroy it.

Such was the strength of the light that it threw long shadows across the ice. Many of the penguins shielded their eyes with their flippers.

'It must have been a terrible burden carrying such an object so far,' whispered Oswain. 'Little wonder so many perished in the task.'

Yarx turned to face the assembly. A wild light gleamed in his eye and at that moment Oswain and Peter knew full well that he was completely mad. For all that, what happened next was quite unexpected.

'There can be only one Master-servant of Shugob,' he cried. 'I, and I alone, have been chosen for that high purpose. There must be no rivals, no possible traitors.' He paused. 'Senators Raaz and Kig have served their part, but the future is not theirs. It belongs to me alone, and to my followers. I give you a supreme Strat order. Slay them both!'

At his words, the Stribs nearest the senators were galvanised into action, as though by a pre-arranged signal. Ice spears flashed and the penguins fell upon the two Strats. Raaz had no chance of wielding the sword, even if he had known how to do so. The odds were overwhelming and, struck from all sides, he collapsed in a heap on the ground.

Kig was more fortunate. Somehow he managed to wriggle free of the mob and, before his assailants could stop him, he was fleeing for his life across the ice. Yarx observed the event with disdain and ordered his Stribs not to bother chasing him. There was plenty of time to deal with Kig later, when Shugob had descended.

The watching companions couldn't believe their eyes. In a matter of seconds one Strat had become a bloodied corpse on the ice and the other had fled. The Stribs resumed their positions, robot-like, as though nothing had happened. Yarx smirked in triumph.

'Now we may proceed,' he declared. With that, he turned to face the South Pole and began to caw a strange, wild incantation.

Andrew and Sarah, though shocked by what had happened, were not slow to grasp the possibilities. They had woken that morning to discover that they were, as Andrew had thought, on the inside of the volcano. Slithering to the floor of the crater, they quickly found where Oswain and Peter were held prisoner but had no idea how they could rescue them. Now Oswain's sword was lying next to Raaz's body.

'We've got to take our chance and get it,' Andrew hissed.

His sister agreed. 'But how? They'll kill us the moment they see us. That Yarx is completely insane!'

'Hmm, it's no use just rushing them, we'd never have enough time,' he replied. 'We need a plan.'

Their problem was solved for them. By some miracle Raaz was still just about alive. They saw him twitch, then grope painfully for the sword. Slowly, he staggered to his feet and, swaying, struggled to lift the weapon in a vain attempt to strike down Lord Yarx. Wide-eyed, the watchers held their breath.

It was no use. Yarx sensed what was happening. Breaking his chant, he turned swiftly and avoided the lethal blow. With a gesture of disgust he ordered the hapless Raaz to be dealt with once and for all. A gap opened in the ranks and the dying penguin was driven through it, before being allowed to fall for the last time on to the ice.

'It's our chance!' gasped Andrew recovering quickly. 'Our only chance.'

The Stribs' eyes were fixed hypnotically on their leader. Plucking up every bit of courage he possessed, Andrew slid from behind the rocks and began to wriggle on his belly towards the stricken Raaz who lay about thirty metres behind the left-hand rank of penguins. Andrew's nerves were at breaking point. One sound, one false movement, and he knew he would be struck by a merciless hail of spears.

'Oh, please, Elmesh, help him!' Sarah prayed.

Oswain stood silent and tense as a bow. Peter was trembling. Everything depended on Andrew's success.

Andrew's progress was agonisingly slow and it seemed to take an age before he reached the sword but, at last, his fingers curled around the hilt. The weapon was heavier than he expected and it tingled in his hand.

His first temptation was to pick it up and run, but he knew he would never make it by panicking. There was only one choice; he had to crawl back the way he had come and hope that no penguin from the far rank facing him would raise the alarm. For just this once he was grateful for Yarx's hypnotic powers.

It was hard work, made even harder by the fear of being spotted. He had never felt as totally exposed as he was out there on the open ice. The moment Yarx finished his chant and the spell was broken, they would see him. Perspiration poured down his face and stung his eyes. Oswain's sword seemed to be growing heavier by the minute.

'Come on, Andrew,' muttered Peter. 'Come on. Faster!'

Time was running out. By the tone of Yarx's voice they

could tell that the incantation was coming to an end. Any moment now and Yarx would cast the key into the channel. Then it would be too late.

He was still ten metres from the pyramid when Yarx finished. At once, a warning cry went up from one of the Strib captains. Andrew leapt to his feet and, dragging the sword, ran slithering and sliding to shelter behind the pyramid. He heard Yarx's harsh screech of rage.

Sarah rushed to her brother's aid. Together, they held the sword and pressed the tip against the base of the pyramid.

'Elmesh! Elmesh!' they cried. 'Let it work. Now!'

The sword immediately blazed bright blue and seemed almost to leap from their hands. Power surged like electricity through its shimmering length. Unable to resist such energy the crystalline prison shattered and fell into a million tiny pieces. Oswain and Peter were free.

'Well done, both of you,' cried Oswain. He seized the sword and bounded straight towards Yarx.

The crazed Strat stood his ground. 'You are too late!' he screamed, holding the fateful key aloft. 'Too late!'

Before Oswain could do anything to stop him, with one wild, maniacal laugh, he hurled the key with all his might at the foot of the South Pole.

21

The Moment of Truth

Oswain froze in mid-stride and stared aghast as the key struck the South Pole. Sparks showered out across the ice in a great golden arc which carried the orange crystal unerringly into the channel cut for it. Ablaze with light, it sped off like a bobsleigh on its fateful journey towards the fiery shaft and the depths of Tergan's lair. No one could stop it now.

It was no time to stand and stare. Ignoring the penguins and their threatening spears. Oswain spun to face his young companions.

'Run for it!' he cried. 'Run for your lives.'

Peter, Sarah and Andrew needed no further urging. They shot off across the ice like scared rabbits. Oswain wasn't far behind.

'As fast as you can,' he panted. 'Don't look back. Just run!'

Fear drove them on. Any moment now and terrible forces would be unleashed upon the world, and they were right in the centre of it all. Ignoring their aching lungs and pounding hearts, they fled from the coming disaster.

Yarx and his followers, however, stood quite unmoved, waiting expectantly as the key careered on its slippery journey towards the hole. Nothing hindered its course; the work had been done well. Yarx glowed with pride. The Masters, Shugob and Tergan, and the Prophetess,

183

Kinera, would reward him well for his service, he felt sure. As for Oswain and the children, they would be dealt with soon enough, when Shugob came!

The channel was cut in a long furrow across the wide icy plain. It took some time for the key to reach its destination. Two minutes passed. The penguins watched patiently as it neared the end of its journey. Then, quite suddenly, it slid out of sight and into the fiery depths where Tergan lay among the burning lava.

For a while there was silence. Then there came a deep subterranean roar which made the ground tremble. Yarx and his followers withdrew from the South Pole to what they supposed was a respectful distance of about fifty paces, and bowed low. The time had come to greet the Masters.

Then, as sudden as a flash of lightning, a brilliant ray of fire blazed from the shaft, lighting up the plain like a gigantic firework going off. It was followed by a fat fountain of white hot lava which boiled out of the ice, turning it through water and into steam in almost an instant. Choking clouds of fog and sulphurous vapour poured in all directions across the plain, enveloping the waiting penguins in sudden grey confusion.

It was the moment of truth. Through Yarx's warped mind flashed memories of his followers who had died needlessly on this mad quest, driven hypnotically by his lust for power and glory, and by the persuasive lies of Kinera. He pushed the thoughts away. Wild-eyed, quite insane, he stood to his feet and cried, 'Welcome, Masters!'

Then, in what he could see were the last seconds of his life, he knew it had all gone wrong. They had been used. Totally deceived. Now it was too late. In the depths of the sulphurous fog he and his followers perished under the merciless flood of heaving white-hot lava that spewed from the earth's bowels and poured across the plain.

A few seconds later and the burning tide hit the South Pole with a deafening roar. The primitive elements met – ice and fire, the coldest and the hottest – and a wild chemistry of doom was unleashed upon the world.

By now the four companions, still running for all they were worth, were over half a kilometre away and had managed to reach some higher ground. The roar hit them like a sledgehammer and they were flung to the ground as though they were no more than rag dolls caught in a hurricane.

'We can go no further,' gasped Oswain. 'Crawl behind those rocks.'

The others, gulping air like stranded fish, followed him. Water was already streaming from the hills around them as the ice melted in the sudden wave of heat. They watched open-mouthed as a broad bank of steam rolled across the plain towards them.

'Those poor, foolish penguins,' Oswain murmured. 'If only they had listened!'

However, he and his companions had no time to think further about the fate of the penguins. From out of the mist a huge column of fire roared upwards into the sky. At once, a strong wind blew up and they were grateful to be in the shelter of the rocks. Everything was being sucked up into the fire – ice, steam, and even the orange cloud which had hung over the mountain. The four companions watched in wonder as the burning column sped straight as an arrow into the suddenly bright blue sky.

As the updraught cleared the air, they could see now that it rose from the South Pole which stood blazing like a brilliant star in the sea of lava around it. Higher and higher the fiery column climbed. Without warning, thunder crashed across the clear heavens, rolling and booming from one horizon to the other. The four friends covered their ears, but nothing could shut out the awful noise.

Then came the event they all feared most. The sky tore open. A terrible black rent, miles across, opened in the heavens. It revealed no stars, only deep, unfathomable darkness.

Sarah screamed and hid her face in her hands. Her dream was coming true. She knew what would happen next.

At that same moment the whole mountain shook with a violent earthquake. Huddled behind the rocks and clutching at one another for dear life, they watched the high cliffs across the crater's plain split with a rending roar into a gigantic open valley to the world beyond. A ripple ran across the plain and then it began to heave and contort as though it were a huge reptile in the throes of death.

'It's the end of the world,' was all Sarah could say.

* * *

On the other side of the mountain, Wheezer and the Ice Maiden were waiting. She sat silent and still with her eyes fixed on the far horizon. Wheezer watched her, scarcely blinking. It was lonely here without the eagles or any of the children. He could feel the back of his neck bristling. It was surely a sign of impending doom; something awful was about to happen.

Then the earth shook. He fluttered off the ground with a wild cry of alarm. The earth tremor was followed by a great crashing roar and, like the others on the inside of the crater, Wheezer saw the terrible column of fire surge into the heavens. For a moment it seemed to him that the volcano was about to erupt.

'Poor Oswain and Peter,' he thought.

He soon realised, however, that this was no ordinary volcanic eruption. In his long years of travel he had seen many, but never anything like this. The pillar of fire rose higher and higher until, with a deafening crash of thunder which sent him squawking to the ground, it pierced the heavens and tore a great hole in the sky. If that wasn't enough, a second earthquake followed almost immediately, leaving the poor pelican whimpering with fear as the mountain split apart right before his eyes.

The Ice Maiden, meanwhile, had remained almost motionless, as though she was quite unaware of what was taking place. Without a sound, she rose, regal in her bearing and aglow with an inner radiance. Her eyes flashed as she glanced first at the torn sky, then at the shattered mountainside. She turned to face the sea and raised her arms, palms outstretched.

'Hail, Naida!' she cried in a loud voice. 'Hail, in a day of doom and glory!'

Wheezer followed her gaze in astonishment.

They came, close-knit, like a shining silver sheet speeding across the ocean, simply myriads upon myriads of tinkling singing lights, all responding to the call of their mistress. They circled around her slender silver and blue figure, then drew themselves into a broad, shimmering train behind her, so that to the entranced Wheezer she seemed like a glorious princess prepared for her coronation. All thought of what else was happening departed from him and he began to feel strangely drowsy.

The Ice Maiden laid her hand gently on his head. At once, he jerked into wakefulness.

'Lest you fall asleep under the Naida's spell and miss all the excitement!' she smiled.

The old pelican bowed low. 'I am your servant, my Lady,' he croaked.

'Then come with us, Wheezer, if you will!' she cried with face aglow. 'We go to meet our destiny.'

Arrayed in splendid light, she walked steadily and effortlessly up towards the great split in the crater wall and to whatever drama awaited within its circle. Wheezer flew on behind, utterly bemused.

'Death or glory, mate,' he muttered to himself. 'That's what it'll be. Death or glory!'

* * *

The earth heaved yet again, but this time more violently than before. With a crashing explosion of fire and rubble, which sent rocks flying everywhere, a scarlet serpentine neck broke the surface. Snorting fire and smoke, a monstrous dragon head reared high in the air. Tergan had at last risen from his long slumber.

The head was followed almost at once by another, and another. Soon, to the horrified gaze of the onlookers, ten fiery horned heads had writhed out of the ground. The children cowered in fear. Tergan was truly terrifying to behold.

The ground continued to heave until it seemed that half the crater floor was going to cave in. A scaly claw broke the surface and, with lava pouring from his armoured hide, the dragon's bloated red body slowly heaved itself from the earth. Tergan was a monster; he must have stood over two hundred metres tall and stretched almost five hundred metres in length.

Defiantly, the great creature reared into the air, and stretched his vast wings. His horned heads reached almost to the crater's rim. Suddenly, he let forth a mighty prehistoric roar and fire belched from each of his ten sabre-toothed mouths.

Then Shugob appeared; a huge orange, ape-like shape clambered through the rent in the sky. Even at that great height the onlookers could see he would more than match Tergan for size. As for danger, it was difficult to say which was worse. Tergan was wild and ferociously evil, but Shugob was returning to avenge his previous defeat. Few could resist his will in the past; he would be even stronger now.

Slowly, the squat figure swung down the column of fire. In spite of his fear, Andrew found himself thinking of a fireman's pole. In just a few minutes Shugob would join Tergan on the island. The choice for all creatures would then be a simple one – serve or die. There would be such deception that children everywhere would serve Shugob and Tergan before they were ever given a chance to know differently.

Peter, Sarah and Andrew were petrified. There was no way of escape and they knew they would be the first to perish.

But Oswain felt none of these things. Steadily, he rose to his feet.

'No, Oswain! No!' cried Sarah in alarm.

Light blazed in his eyes and his features were set. Oswain knew what he was doing. The hour had come. Slowly, he raised his sword. Light poured from its length and seemed to pierce the smoky gloom of the crater. Like a beam of bright sunshine breaking through the rain clouds it blazed across the valley, clean and clear, bringing freshness and hope.

That hope sprang at once to the children's hearts – and then they saw something truly wonderful. The Ice Maiden, Loriana, Mistress of the Mountains, emerged from between the broken boulders and cliffs adorned in a shimmering silver cloud of resplendent majesty. Oswain was suddenly bathed in light – not silver, but burning like fire. He cried strongly, 'Hail, noble Lady! Our hour has come!'

They heard her clear voice return, pure and sweet, 'Hail, my Lord! It has come indeed!'

22

The Voice of Shugob

Shugob looked down upon the world with grim satisfaction. A few puffs of cloud drifted below him, floating like icebergs on the bland grey sea; further away more cloud, like driven snow piled high, half hid distant lands from his view. But they were all there – the lands, the peoples, the children – and soon they would be his.

Smug with the success of his plans, he continued his steady descent from the howling black wastes above to the unsuspecting earth below. The island was in view, a dun coloured, surf-washed shape from which rose the fiery column that had made his entrance into the world possible. He could see Tergan. Even from this height his ruddy form was unmistakable. Shugob grimaced with pleasure. His ancient ally was awake – and how he had grown!

The woman, Kinera, would be awaiting him. He pondered what reward he would bestow upon her. Perhaps it would be enough that she would see the spirits of children sucked dry – she who had corrupted her own son and lost him, and who now wished vengeance on the whole world! Well, Shugob would grant her vengeance in full measure.

That was not all he saw. An unexpected gleam, a clearer light, some hateful purity, caught his eye and furrowed his hideous brow. This, decidedly, was not in harmony with his plans. Was he to be opposed the moment he arrived? Why had Tergan not seen this and dealt with it? Shugob hastened his descent. There was no time to lose admiring the scenery.

He hit the world with bone-jarring force – one foot on the island, the other in the sea – and towered over the island, high above even the monstrous Tergan. The dragon reared his swaying body in welcome and let out a fire-spattered prehistoric roar. Ancient hunger and vicious power were met together. They would serve one another's needs well. Shugob bellowed a welcome in return and the air trembled as though nature itself feared what was to come.

Shugob turned his attention to the splendid light which Oswain and Loriana shared across the valley floor. It spelt another kind of power; dangerous, the kind that might threaten all his plans.

He spoke.

To Peter, Sarah and Andrew, cowering in fear and wonder behind the rocks, his voice sounded like the throaty roaring of a lion, but in their minds they could hear something quite different. The words shocked them.

'So, you are named Oswain?' The tone was unexpectedly educated and reasonable. 'And you are Loriana? Interesting. I see you are not the common kind, for you possess those special gifts of mind and spirit given only to the few. It is good that you are here, for you may be precisely the ones we are seeking to join us in our Great Purpose.'

'What a cheek!' gasped Sarah. 'How dare he even suggest it! And how does he know their names?'

'Ah, children, too,' the voice continued smoothly. 'No

need to hide, my dears, for nothing is hidden from
Shugob, is it? I can see everything. Absolutely everything.'

Sarah felt herself blush. Her defences were stripped
away under Shugob's penetrating gaze and she was made
to feel weak and foolish. Her two brothers felt the same.
All their hidden thoughts and feelings seemed exposed to
his menacing presence, and there was nowhere to hide.
All three wanted to cry.

'You will join me, of course,' Shugob continued, his
voice now firm. His tone and awesome presence
appeared to allow no argument.

However, Oswain was put off neither by the size nor
the impudence of Shugob. His voice sounded weak and
thin by comparison, but there was no mistaking his spirit.

'We do not use our powers to serve evil. If we are not
hidden from you, then you also know that your plans are
not hidden from us. We understand full well what lies
behind your promises of peace and prosperity!'

'Hurrah for Oswain!' cried Peter.

Then Tergan spoke. His voice was terrible, harsh and
wheezing, desolate, like a bleak winter wind in a hollow
place. Death was in every breath, hopelessness in every
word.

'You challenge the will of Shugob? Then you challenge
mine also. I will not make you so fair an offer. I do not
invite you to join us; instead, I command you to serve us.
Your powers, your lives, your minds and your spirits
shall be given to Shugob, or I shall destroy you.'

Faint across the valley, but in spirit strong enough to
reach their ears came the voice of Loriana in reply.

'You do not frighten us, Shugob. You were once before

vanquished in shame and defeat, and now you dare to return! Do not expect to win this time round, either. As for you, Tergan, you may be grown in size, but not in grace or wisdom. Your threats will not change our minds!'

At this, one of Tergan's great heads bent low. He leered at the Ice Maiden with a gleaming eye.

'A pretty maiden, a dragon's desire,' he gloated. 'Long shall I torment you before at length I devour you, even to your very soul!'

'Do not be hasty, Tergan,' came Shugob's silky voice. 'Persuasion before force. Who better than these to serve our will, if they may be won over. They love children! Imagine how easily their charm and magic would win the lives of little followers everywhere. Then there will be common wenches enough, and children too, to satisfy your hungers and desires.'

'Ugh, I hate him,' cried Sarah. 'I hate you!' she screamed.

At once, she felt Shugob's presence fill her mind.

'You will be the first to serve me, little one,' he said. 'Already you have been party to my plans, Strib 616! The way is open for me to take you completely.'

Sarah could do nothing to resist the hypnotic will of Shugob. Her mind filled with evil and disgusting pictures. Vile thoughts poured through her brain. At first she hated them, but to her own shame she began to like what she was seeing. A moment more and she knew the shame would fade, and she would be his – and then her spirit would begin to drain away until she was a person without hope or purpose to her life.

Dimly she heard a cry.

'No!'

It was Oswain's voice.

'As I thought,' said Shugob. 'You would not want her changed against her will. Then follow me! I offer you power, and a rule of peace and plenty. After all, you are a king. We will give the children all that they think they want. They will be happy. Is that not your desire?'

'Happy, yes, but no longer free to choose anything or any future except what you offer,' responded Oswain. 'And all the time you would feed on their spirits to nourish your own perverse cravings. You are a parasite! Just look what happened to the penguins.'

'Ah, yes, the penguins. Foolish creatures, weren't they? A mere means to an end. But you are different. You I would honour, if you honour me,' answered Shugob. 'Understand that I want you with me. You are in harmony with the hidden powers. Surely all such should unite? Who is there to say otherwise?'

'We worship Elmesh alone,' came the Ice Maiden's curt reply. 'That is already known to you. Why do you dare challenge it? All powers are not the same simply because they are powers. Some are good and some are evil. They do not mix!'

'I hate Elmesh,' rasped Tergan as though pricked by her words. 'Long ago he banished me. Do you presume him powerful enough to stop me, now that I am full grown? I spit on Elmesh! I despise his ways!'

At which a great slug of molten fire spewed from one of the dragon's mouths and spattered against a rock face near the Ice Maiden. She did not even flinch.

'Your blasphemy will not go unpunished,' cried Oswain. 'Neither threats of death nor smooth words shall bend our wills. Elmesh lives, and in his name we withstand you. Go from this world. Return to the darkness from where you were hatched, both of you!'

At this Shugob's tone changed. Fury was in his voice – crushing, overwhelming rage. Reasonableness was at an end.

'Then you shall be the first example of what happens to those who rebel against the new age we bring. Die Oswain! Die Loriana – you and your snivelling brats. Let your last thought be that others shall have the honour which might have been yours.'

So saying, he raised a gigantic foot to crush them. It was so large that the sun was almost blotted out, and the children felt the cold shadow of death pass over them.

Oswain's sword seemed suddenly to grow in his hand. Its length blazed in a beam of searing light that struck the sole of the monster's foot even as it descended. Shugob howled with unexpected pain and rage and hopped off wildly into the sea, creating great waves where his feet splashed.

It might as well have been a signal, for as he did so, the skies were filled with a terrible screeching sound. The clouds themselves appeared to be shrieking above their heads. Peter, Sarah and Andrew covered their ears, but heedless of the danger rose awestruck to their feet.

Then the clouds were revealed for what they were. Arca had returned, and with him not hundreds but many thousands of shining white eagles. They swooped on the monster, throwing him into complete confusion as he sought to swipe them away. With a cry of rage he clutched the fiery pillar and clambered up high off the earth as fast as he could in an effort to escape their fury.

Loriana wasted no time. With the Naida forming a

protective cloak around her, she raced across the crater floor to where Oswain stood in warrior-stance keenly watching the aerial battle.

Now Tergan was roused. With earth-jarring steps he advanced on them and death was in his many eyes. His fiery-jowled heads snapped and dripped great gobbets of fire.

A head lunged for Oswain who parried with a swift blow and again the blade forged by Elmesh grew and blazed. Fire struck fire and with a howl of pain and a mighty crash the great head fell lifeless to the ground.

Another snapped and snarled at the Ice Maiden. But it was only to feel the freezing power of the Naida. One touch from the shimmering lights and the fire-breathing head turned blue, shrivelled to a reptilian skull, and then shattered to pieces.

Eight heads remained. One went for Oswain. Again he struck. Another seized a great rock in its teeth and would have hurled it upon them, but the Naida were too quick and it met the same frozen fate as the other.

Again and again the fearsome, fire-spewing heads lunged for Oswain and Loriana. But nothing could break the power of the Naida or resist the sting of Oswain's sword. Head after head fell. Meanwhile, the eagles continued to drive Shugob higher and higher into the sky and back to the darkness from where he had come. Peter, Sarah and Andrew watched anxiously from the shelter of the rocks. There was nothing else they could do in the face of such a titanic conflict.

Only three of Tergan's heads remained and it seemed that what cunning he possessed was concentrated in those heads. He could see that for all their might, his enemies were tiring. One head hovered, weaving on its long neck over the Ice Maiden, spitting fire but keeping just out of reach. Another twisted and turned, trying to find a way of striking Oswain but remaining out of range of his sword. It was a tactic designed to tire his foes – and to distract them.

The third head searched out Peter, Sarah and Andrew. Great teeth picked up rocks and threw them aside. The children, powerless to do anything, could feel the fiery stench of his sulphurous breath as he reared above them.

'Oswain, help!' Sarah cried in desperation.

Oswain, seeing what was happening and unmindful of his own danger, ran to their aid. The dragon laughed harshly. He had caught his foe off guard. With the merest flick of his neck he sent Oswain tumbling and stunned to the ground. The sword fell from his grasp and lodged uselessly among the rocks.

'Now which shall I have first, the man, the maid, or the children?' mused the dragon.

Then he commanded, 'Call off the eagles!'

Loriana sighed. Oswain was down and weaponless. The children were in deadly peril. She whistled loud and clear.

At once, the eagles drew back from Shugob, leaving him tattered and torn, but still very much alive. He clambered back down the fiery column until he hovered above the dragon.

'You have done well, Tergan,' he growled. 'We have them in our power. Now let us decide how we shall use that power to our best advantage.'

Dragons are not good at being reasonable. Tergan was overcome by something more powerful than Shugob's words. Memories of his horrid past came flooding back. He was hungry for children, and that hunger could no longer wait. Heedless of the stupidity of losing hostages with which he and Shugob might have bargained, the great head reared. In seconds the children would perish.

Peter, Sarah and Andrew knew it. Gripping each other's hands tightly, together and unprotected, with upturned faces they courageously awaited their fate.

Just as all seemed lost, a wild cry rent the air. Tergan hesitated for a moment. Peter, Sarah and Andrew spun round and stared.

A small figure was running towards them, as swift and fleet-footed as an antelope, leaping and scrambling over the rocks. They could hardly believe what they were seeing.

'It's Rag!' gasped Peter. 'Look!'

They watched in amazement as he raced to where Oswain lay. Without hesitation the boy seized the fallen sword and with it turned to face the mighty dragon.

Tergan hissed angrily, and then snorted with scorn. Another child for lunch!

Rag held the sword outstretched in both hands and began to whirl round. It looked like a wild dervish dance as he span. Faster and faster he turned until he was no more than a blur to his onlookers.

Then, suddenly, he let fly the sword. It sped through the air like a burning meteorite, and before Tergan could so much as move, the shining blade buried itself deep in his bloated belly.

Rag may or may not have known what made the dragon's body so huge. Tergan was not all flesh and bone but possessed instead a vast body cavity which was filled with inflammable marsh gas. That is why he could breathe out fire – and why what happened next was almost unavoidable.

Tergan, with a roar of rage, turned a head to pluck the sword from his belly, and as he did so, fire from his mouth ignited the leaking gas. At once, a terrible flame spurted from his side.

The beleaguered company watched in wonder as the jet of flame burned brighter and brighter. The dragon began furiously to flap his huge wings in an effort to put it out, but that only made matters worse. He rose crazily from the ground, blotting out the light as he hovered above them.

It was his fatal mistake; Tergan's great hulk now began to behave the way a party balloon does when you blow it up and let go of the end. Completely out of control, he suddenly went soaring and spinning off into the sky to where Shugob still clung to his fiery column.

Unable to stop himself, the dragon struck the great orange monster full in the chest.

'No! No!' roared Shugob.

It was too late. Tergan exploded into a huge roaring fire-ball that totally engulfed both monsters. Whether it was due to the power of Oswain's sword or to some other force, nobody knew, but the heat produced was so terrible, so intense, that it utterly consumed them.

The onlookers cowered as the explosion echoed through the heavens. The shock-wave hit them like the blast of a furnace. Then, silently and solemnly, they rose to their feet to watch as the fireball slowly traced a majestic arc across the sky before plunging with a harmless splash into the distant ocean.

23

Tergan's Hidden Treasure

For a long time everyone simply stood and stared. No one spoke, nobody moved. The monsters were gone and their evil alliance thwarted. It was almost too much to believe.

At length, Oswain spoke quietly. 'Elmesh be praised,' he said. 'Victory is ours.'

Andrew could contain himself no longer. 'Yeee-haaaahhh!!' he cried, waving his fists in the air. 'Yeah! Yeah! Yeah! Sorted! Shugob's sorted. Tergan's terminated!'

The others laughed.

'Yes, and all because of Rag. What a shot!' Peter exclaimed. 'Talk about scoring the winning goal!'

Rag stood there grinning from ear to ear. 'Me used to practise knocking apples off tree like that,' he explained. 'Tergan big apple!'

'You were fantastic,' said Sarah. 'Absolutely brilliant and marvellous and amazing.' Before he could so much as move she placed a big kiss on his cheek, which made him blush.

'Yes,' said Oswain. 'There's no doubt about it, Rag, you are the hero of the day. I'm not sure what would have happened if you hadn't turned up when you did. You were the last person I expected to see,' he added.

'You did not go with the eagles, did you?' said the Ice Maiden. 'I thought not.'

He looked at her thoughtfully for a moment to see if she was angry, but then said, 'Me stay. 'Cos me want to fight dragon. And . . . and I want help my . . . my friends. I not have many friends.'

'Well, you're our friend, for always,' Peter said and he slapped him on the back. His brother and sister nodded their heads vigorously.

'Ours, too,' Oswain added with a smile.

'Well, friends all, it's time we caught up with one another's adventures,' the Ice Maiden suggested. 'There seem to have been a lot of heroes in the past few hours.'

With the noonday sun warming them, they walked a little way above the jumbled mess of the crater floor and sat down to relate all that had happened. Wheezer got special mention for his bravery in the face of the vultures.

'Just done what I should,' he coughed. 'Getting a bit old for all this sort of thing, though.'

'Sarah and Andrew rescued us from the pyramid,' said Peter.

'Ah yes,' Loriana said. 'A courageous thing to do, especially when you have first to climb such a mountain in the dark.'

'You knew we hadn't gone with the eagles, didn't you?' said Sarah.

She nodded.

'Then why didn't you stop us, or tell us off?'

The Ice Maiden gazed at them thoughtfully. 'Sometimes, just sometimes, it is right to disobey. It must never be for selfish ends, and even when you do you must be prepared to face the consequences. No one else must be blamed if you fall into trouble. But you may – on occasions you must – go against orders if the cause is sufficiently noble.'

'I wanted to save Oswain and Peter, even if I died,' said Sarah.

'Me too,' said Andrew.

'I know,' replied the Ice Maiden, with a look that said she really did understand, and approved.

'It was scary, though,' Andrew explained. 'We were half dead by the time we reached the top, and then we . . .' His mouth dropped open. 'Then we met Kinera. I'd forgotten about her. Where is she?'

'She chased us down the mountain and kept changing into a weasel or something, but then we caught her,' Sarah explained. 'We tangled her up with her lyre, but it wouldn't have held her for long.'

'Anyway, she must have escaped because we heard music when the penguins came out this morning,' said Andrew. 'She's got to be around somewhere.'

Their conversation was interrupted at that moment by the cries of Arca and his eagles. In their relief over the destruction of Shugob and Tergan, everyone had forgotten about the column of fire, yet, across the crater's floor it still blazed into the heavens and out through the great tear in the sky. They turned now to see thousands of white eagles circling round it. Closer and closer they drew until it looked as though the fiery pillar was entirely covered in cotton wool.

'Oh no, they'll be killed!' gasped Sarah.

They were not. Instead, the thronging eagles gleamed brighter and brighter until the light was almost too great for the eyes to bear. Then, at some hidden signal, ablaze with light, the eagles flew outwards and upwards to form a vast canopy of dazzling whiteness. To the amazement of the watchers, the pillar of fire was simply no more. *Tons better than an aircraft display*, Andrew thought.

Minutes later, Arca appeared swooping over the rim of the crater towards them. He held something in his talons.

Everyone present greeted him with applause as, with the merest breath of air, the great eagle landed.

'You have served Elmesh well,' he cawed. 'All is not yet restored but the battle is won.'

The onlookers heard what he said, but their eyes were on the limp bundle that he dropped at their feet. A golden-haired weasel groaned and flinched and then, before their startled gaze, transformed into a bedraggled woman. Defeat was written across her face.

She gazed up at Oswain. 'So, command him to kill me. As you did my son,' she said.

Oswain looked puzzled. 'I do not understand,' he said.

Andrew tugged at his sleeve. 'Sarah and I do,' he said. 'She told us last night. Her son was Zarbid.'

Oswain addressed the woman. 'Is this true?'

'The boy is telling the truth,' she replied.

'Zarbid – your son – did much evil in Traun and brought war against my lands. He made human sacrifices and would have killed the Ice Maiden. He tried to have King Surin assassinated. Yet I did not order his death. I have no command over the eagles that descended upon Traun, for they have their own reasons and keep their own counsels. It is in their nature to destroy evil and they do not feel loss as we do,' Oswain explained.

The woman looked bitterly at Arca. 'Then he had better destroy me, hadn't he?' she said. 'I am surely as evil as my son.'

'It would not please Elmesh,' Arca cawed.

'Why not? It pleased him before, didn't it?' She rounded on Oswain. 'You cannot know the pain of a mother's loss,' she said.

'True enough,' he answered. 'Yet I saw the one I once loved – Dorinda – totally corrupted because of what you did.'

'But you have found another love.' Kinera looked at the Ice Maiden. 'I can have no more children.'

Loriana stooped down beside the woman. 'I am sorry that you suffered such a loss,' she said. 'Mothers bear their sons in pain. They seldom find them evil, whatever they do. Yet vengeance is no answer. Bitterness in your spirit will destroy you, and it might have destroyed tens of thousands of mother's sons and daughters had Shugob succeeded.' She looked closely at Kinera. 'I do not think that you are wholly evil,' she said.

Defeat hung from the woman's slumped shoulders like a lead blanket. 'It was not always like this,' she whispered, almost to herself. 'Once I wished to help people. I wanted to use my music to bring happiness and peace – but life turned a different corner and I walked where I should not have.' She lifted her head. 'Once I wanted to be with you, Oswain.'

'Maybe that was when it all started.'

She sighed. 'No, before that. When I saw them kill Elmesh.'

Oswain shook his head slowly. 'No,' he said softly. 'You saw what they wanted you to see. What appeared to die was the twisted idea of Elmesh that they had taught you. The real Elmesh, full of love and truth and kindness did not die, and cannot die.'

Sarah reached out her hand and clasped Kinera's. 'I know you have lost everything,' she said. 'It must feel really awful, but we don't hate you. I hope that you will be able to find happiness again.'

The woman gave Sarah a watery smile. 'You are young, but you are also kind,' she said. 'It will take time. That's all I can say.'

'Stay with us,' Oswain offered.

Kinera shrugged. 'For the moment, I have little choice,' she said.

Oswain turned to Arca, sensing that the eagle was restless. The Ice Maiden helped Kinera to her feet and led her away.

'We must thank you again for your part in the cause of freedom,' Oswain said to the eagle. 'It was nobly done and we honour you and your company.'

'And wonderful at the end,' Sarah piped up. She always felt a special bond with Arca.

The eagle looked kindly upon her. 'It is only fitting that we should fight to protect the children. But we thank you, Sarah.'

'I've never seen so many of your kind,' she said. 'Not even when you were at the cleansing of Traun.'

'That was small compared to the powers which Shugob possessed,' he answered. 'You know little of how much turned on this battle. It required a great muster from many lands.'

'Where are they going now?' Andrew wanted to know.

Arca's eye rose. 'Not all clouds are clouds,' he said, with what might almost have been the hint of a smile.

In the far-off heights, the canopy of eagles might easily have been mistaken for no more than a patch of cloud.

'Now I go to join them But I give you two last words: look for the casket of gold; and he who is ruined may still be saved. Farewell, servants of Elmesh – until we meet once more.'

With that, their mighty friend and ally rose from the earth and sped into the white cloudy distance. They stared until even the keenest eye could no longer distinguish him.

'Isn't he wonderful?' sighed Sarah. 'I've always loved Arca.'

'What did he mean, look for the casket of gold?' asked Peter.

'Why, it's obvious, silly,' Andrew answered. 'All dragons collect treasure, don't they? There must be some priceless hoard that Tergan has been hiding all these years.'

'I'll take a look, if you like,' Wheezer offered. 'Long as I don't get my tail singed, that is.'

With that, the pelican flew off in a sweeping search over the smouldering plain. He was soon back.

'Found it,' he gasped. 'Not far away at all. And the ground looks cool.'

'We'll go carefully for all that,' Oswain replied with feeling.

It took almost half an hour to pick their way across the crater, and they found that they were not so very far from where the South Pole stood. The pole was beginning to reassert its power over the underground fire and the ground was quite cool again.

Peter spotted it first; a gleaming yellow casket lay half buried in the ash and lava. Everyone rushed towards it.

'It's not all that big,' was Andrew's first comment.

'I bet it's still full of the most priceless treasure,' said Sarah.

'Can I open it?' Peter asked.

Oswain nodded and they all watched – Andrew and Sarah a little impatiently it has to be said – as Peter wrestled with the hasp. Then it was free, and slowly he drew back the lid.

What greeted their eyes, however, was not a pile of glittering gold and jewels, but an ancient-looking book with a worn leather cover. The children's faces dropped with dismay.

Oswain, however, stooped and lifted it reverently from the casket.

'Treasure indeed,' sighed the Ice Maiden.

He nodded silently, then said, 'Maybe this is what was really at stake all the time.'

In answer to the children's questioning glances he showed them the title.

'The Tale of the Seven Rainbows,' read Sarah.

'The Book of Truth. There is no more precious find than this,' Oswain explained. 'It was known to have vanished long ago, but nobody was sure what had happened to it. Many thought it perished when the island sank. Now we know – now at last we know for sure. Tergan has sat on it all these years.'

'But what is it?' asked Peter

'This book contains the secret of happiness,' he replied. 'For in this is stored the true wisdom of Elmesh. We must guard it and see it safely back to our realms where the pages will be read and studied with delight.'

'Can't we read it now?' Peter asked. 'I mean, if it's so wonderful, I'd like to see what it says.'

Oswain looked at him thoughtfully, then shook his head.

'The Book of Truth is not like other books,' he said. 'Only if you have the heart of a true seeker can you understand its meaning. Curiosity is not enough. And it tests your heart at every page to know whether you still wish to seek for truth. If not, then it becomes closed to you. I do not think you are ready at this moment, Peter.'

'Can't I just take a look?'

Oswain relented, shrugged his shoulders and obliged.

Peter opened the book at random. A faint rainbow haze hung over the page. Peter blinked, but the words seemed very ordinary indeed – just some boring old stories about people with funny names.

'Hmm, I suppose you're right,' he said, a trifle glumly, and he handed the volume back.

'I'm sure we could understand it if we were in the enchanted glade back in the Great Forest,' Sarah said. 'We are going there soon, aren't we? I'm really looking forward to meeting Mr and Mrs Trotter again, and all our other friends.'

'Surely you would understand the book in the enchanted glade, Sarah,' said Loriana. 'But I have a feeling you are not to return there on this occasion. There are things amiss which must first be remedied.'

Sarah looked crestfallen, and a little alarmed. 'What do you mean?' she said.

'Have you looked up?'

Only then did it dawn on the children that although the pillar of fire had gone, the black hole was still in the sky. It had been hidden behind the white canopy created by the eagles, but they were no longer there and the tear was clearly visible, even in daylight. They noticed something else, too. A dark smoke was pouring through and drifting across the high heavens.

'What's that?' asked Andrew.

'That,' said Oswain, 'is bad news. Shugob may be gone but his madness has let in other evils. Loriana is right, there will be much work needed to restore the damage.'

'Can't anything be done to stop it getting worse?' Sarah asked, by now thoroughly alarmed.

'There is hope, strong hope,' the Ice Maiden answered. 'We shall wait, and see what happens tonight.'

That is what they did. After returning to the beach, where it was warmer, they sat and waited, watching as the sun slowly sank into the sea and the first stars lit up the deepening blue afterglow. Sips from the Ice Maiden's cordial sustained them in their vigil.

Night came. Stars filled the sky, but the black tear was unmistakable. Not a single star gleamed from where it stretched across the velvet heaven.

Sarah was deeply troubled by it all. She left the others and went for a walk along the beach. 'Please, Elmesh, make it go away,' she prayed.

She glanced up. The hole was still there. Glumly, kicking idly at the sand as she walked, she began to retrace her steps. *If only they could do something*, she thought.

Then a gleam caught her eye. It was low on the horizon but she had little doubt about it at all. Her heart gave a little skip of joy. Elrilion, the star of Elmesh, was rising. How long it seemed since last she had seen it. Excitedly, she ran back to the others.

'Ah,' said the Ice Maiden smiling. 'See how beautifully it shines. Do you not feel hope and joy once more?'

Together they watched, as slowly the star rose in the sky. They marvelled how its limpid light far outshone all the others.

'It's going to touch that hole,' gasped Sarah after a while. 'Look. Its path will take it straight into it.'

Sure enough it did. But to the delight of the onlookers, instead of the star vanishing, the black hole began slowly but surely to close up. Within the space of an hour there was no sign of it at all and the whole sky blazed with the glory of the stars as though in honour of Elrilion, whose splendour seemed greater than ever.

'Now we can rest at peace,' said Oswain at last. 'Sleep safely, children. While Elrilion shines you need have no fear of the darkness.'

24

Journeys Home

'Good morning, your honourable Majesties, and other personages present!'

The squawking voice woke the children up at once. Peter blinked in the grey light of dawn.

'Who's that?' he groaned.

'Dunno,' mumbled Andrew. 'But they're a right pest, whoever they are.'

The unexpected guest who had disturbed their slumbers turned out to be none other than Wheezer's companion at the beginning of the adventure, Horatio the Third – whom the children had not, of course, met before.

'Hey, it's a puffin,' laughed Sarah. 'How sweet!'

'So it is,' said Peter. 'Complete with bowler hat and umbrella!'

'He looks pretty wet, though,' Andrew observed.

The highly formal Horiato was most offended by their comments and puffed out his chest with an indignant 'Hrrumph'. But the effect was rather lost on the children because he really was in a rather bedraggled state. They just couldn't help laughing.

'I can see little to laugh about,' he began. 'If you had seen the way . . .'

He was interrupted by Oswain. 'Ah, Horatio, no less. We were wondering when you might arrive. Did you have a good journey?'

The puffin bowed low. 'Your Majesty, I was just saying . . .'

'That you are entitled to a little more respect and that you've had a very wet journey indeed,' Oswain laughed. 'You have my most sincere commiserations, sir. However, compared to what these good folk have endured, you may count yourself fortunate to have suffered so little. Less pomp, Horatio! Treat real heroes as they deserve.'

The puffin spluttered and coughed a bit, then mumbled something like, 'If you say so, your Majesty.'

Horatio's early arrival soon had them on their feet and before long the sun was rising to herald a beautifully clear day. One glance at the cloudless sky told them that the hole really had been well and truly repaired; everyone was relieved to see that not even a trace remained.

Sarah looked round for Kinera. She was nowhere to be seen.

'She's gone, then?' she asked the Ice Maiden.

Loriana nodded. 'Yes.'

'You know, I felt really sorry for her in the end. It's like, well, she's done a lot of bad things, but she's lost everything. She looked very sad . . . or . . . or was that just an act?' she asked.

'I think perhaps that we saw her as she really is,' Loriana answered. 'We shall see.'

'Do you think people like her, you know, liars, can really change?'

'What do you think, Sarah?'

'I hope so,' the girl answered.

'Sometimes, as with Surin, it is very sudden. For others, it is a longer journey. Kinera is a traveller. Maybe in her travels she will find healing. Let us pray so,' said the Ice Maiden.

The little company had slept on the beach under a sheltered ledge not far from the remains of the jungle. Unfortunately, in spite of searching all around, even Rag had not been able to find any surviving trees. So it was the Ice Maiden's cordial again for breakfast. 'Satisfying,' whispered Andrew. 'But I'd really like cornflakes, and fried egg, and sausages, and beans, and . . .'

'Well, Horatio, tell us your tale,' said Oswain. 'What news do you bring?'

'I have come from the Great Forest,' he began. 'By air and by sea. The latter part of my journey has been most uncomfortable and wet, as you can see. But I was simply following my orders which I received from Trotter – at great personal inconvenience, I may add.'

Oswain gave him a stern look from under lowered brows.

'Oh, how is Trotter?' Sarah asked anxiously. 'Is he all right?'

'He has been very busy with the refugee animals and he has spent many hours in the enchanted glade,' replied the puffin. 'I believe he is well, but he looks concerned. "Much to be mended," is all he keeps muttering. "Much to be mended".'

'Trotter discerns the future,' interjected the Ice Maiden. 'I suppose he has already seen the destruction of Shugob and Tergan. But he senses there will be problems because of the torn sky. Oswain, you must soon return to the Great Forest. You are needed there.'

'I do have some good news,' said Horatio. 'Mrs Trotter has become a celebrity.'

'Really?'

All eyes were on the puffin and, relishing an audience, he told them of Mrs Trotter's encounter with Kinera and of how she rescued the children of Elmar.

'Good for her,' said Oswain. 'I've always thought there was more to Mrs Trotter than meets the eye.'

'So that was why I saw a vision of her when I was rescuing you from Kinera's control,' laughed the Ice Maiden.

'I want to ask her how she did it,' said Andrew.

Oswain smiled. 'I am sure you do,' he said. 'But I'm afraid it will have to be some other time.'

'You mean, we're not going back with you?' Sarah had tears in her eyes.

Oswain smiled. 'I would love you to come, Sarah, but I sense it is time for you to return to your own realm. Maybe we shall meet again soon. Meanwhile, Horatio has brought transport to return you home. Take a look.'

Oswain pointed out to sea. There, lying offshore and bobbing in the breakers, was a small raft.

'That!' exclaimed Peter.

'You have not seen everything,' laughed Loriana. 'Look, some friends from the past have arrived.'

Even as she spoke several slick grey heads bobbed out of the water, and above the gentle lapping of the waves there rose a deep cello-like song.

'Hail, worthy heralds of victory! Hail, lords and ladies of the light!'

'It's the dolphins!' exclaimed Sarah. 'They must be the ones who rescued us from Gublak's island. Don't you remember?'

She ran to the water's edge and waved vigorously to

their old friends while the dolphins leapt and cavorted in the waves, much to the delight of all who watched. Then their leader swam near and in his deep musical voice, which so charmed the ears of the listeners, said, 'Again we meet, though on another shore, yet fair are your faces still. The victors we salute, and in our homage offer service for your journey home.'

'Can we ride all the way home on their backs then?' Sarah asked. Her eyes were shining with excitement.

'All the way home?' Oswain murmured with a faraway look in his eyes. 'Yes. Though it will not take you long. Do not fear the way.'

Peter looked at Oswain oddly for a moment, and then asked, 'What will happen now?'

'The island of Aethius will sink,' said Oswain.

'What, for ever?'

'You never quite know with islands like this,' he replied.

'But what are the rest of you going to do?' Andrew wanted to know.

'Oh, Rag and I will ride together. I must return him safely to his family. The eagles will have taken all the other children home by now and his parents will be worried about him – though they probably know he can look after himself better than most.' Oswain laughed. 'The raft is for us. One of the dolphins will take us in tow. And Horatio will come, too. I have things to discuss with him!'

The puffin looked decidedly uncomfortable at the thought.

'Me have much to tell my family,' grinned Rag. 'I glad to go home now.'

'What about you, Loriana?' asked Sarah. 'Are you going with Oswain?'

The Ice Maiden smiled. 'It is my heart's desire, of course, but you have forgotten something Sarah. There is the little matter of the South Pole. Somebody must return it to its rightful place. I think I should do that, don't you?'

Andrew asked Wheezer what his plans were and Oswain offered him a welcome for ever in the Great Forest or any of his domains.

'I think I shall fly round the world one more time,' replied the old bird. 'Never could settle in one place. But I shall have a tale or two to tell on some far-off archipelago, of that you may be sure. And I shall always remember you, every one of you.' His eyes glistened wistfully behind his battered spectacles.

Aware that the time for sad partings had come, Oswain suggested that they make a last journey together back to the crater in order to see the Ice Maiden on her way. So, with the consent of the dolphins, who said they would be honoured to wait for their guests, the party set off up the hillside.

They had just come in sight of the South Pole when a faint cry reached their ears. Everyone turned at the unexpected sound. There, limping and stumbling towards them over the rough ground, was a very bruised and battered emperor penguin. He looked in a most sorry state, but Sarah recognised him at once.

'It's Kig!' she cried, and drew back in concern. Was all this evil not done with yet?

Oswain eyed the penguin keenly. Forgetting for a moment that the scabbard was empty, he reached for his sword, but Loriana stayed his hand.

'I think he is no longer any threat. Remember Arca's words,' she murmured. And with that, she went to meet the penguin. The others watched as a serious conversation took place. At last, she and Kig returned to the company. Kig's eyes were downcast. He came straight up to Oswain and bowed low.

'I have been given over to evil ways,' he croaked. 'Evil beyond measure. I am a fool and I should die, for others were sacrificed to a cause which I now know was false. My life is in your hands.'

'And so it shall remain,' said Oswain sternly, 'for I charge you before these witnesses, Kig, to return to your kinsfolk and to teach them the ways of truth. Should you ever again rebel, understand that your life shall be forfeit.'

'I thank you, sir,' said the penguin. 'I thank you for your mercy.'

In this the children saw the true greatness and wisdom of the Lord Oswain, for Kig did return, and he was to teach his kind never again to seek corrupt powers. So from that day on, the penguins remained creatures of peace and happiness.

The Ice Maiden spoke. 'Kig shall journey with me and he will learn many lessons from my lips. It will not be safe for the rest of you to come further now, so we must take our leave.'

With that she bade the children an affectionate farewell and kissed Oswain.

'I shall soon return, my love,' she cried. 'Await my coming!'

Fifteen minutes later, they watched in wonder as the Naida came at her call and descended shimmering upon the South Pole. Then she was lifted from the ground, along with the repentant penguin, who now slept under their influence. Gracefully, she alighted on the glittering star which topped the pole. Then slowly it rose, splendid in the morning light, and borne by the tinkling bell-like song of the Naida, drifted across the crater's rim and disappeared southwards out of sight.

Sarah was weeping. 'Oh, I do hate saying goodbye,' she sniffed.

Just then an earth tremor reminded them sharply that they had little time left on this island. They hurried back to the sea where the dolphins patiently awaited their return.

The three children were soon astride their willing bearers and Oswain, Rag and Horatio were aboard the raft. Peter saw that Oswain clasped the golden casket with its precious contents. He felt that he would like to understand it some time soon.

'We go different ways,' cried Oswain across the water. 'Farewell, and do not be afraid.'

Then they were off. In no time at all the raft was out of sight, as was the island. Wheezer stayed with them for a while but, with a haunting farewell cry, soon soared away on his endless circuit of the seas. Only the children were left, speeding across a vast and featureless ocean to the comfortable humming of the dolphins.

'This is great!' cried Peter. 'But where are we going?'

'Dunno,' shouted Andrew in answer. 'Why did Oswain tell us not to be afraid? What's going to happen?'

They didn't have to wait long for an answer, for a few minutes later, without any warning, all three were suddenly and unceremoniously flicked from the backs of the dolphins and into the water.

'Hey,' gasped Andrew spluttering to the surface. 'What's the idea?'

'Goodbye,' sang the dolphins. 'Here we leave you, but do not fear. Elmesh will see you safe.'

'You can't leave us in the middle of the ocean,' cried Sarah. 'We'll drown!'

But the dolphins were already gone.

All three could swim well and trod water together.

'What are we going to do?' Peter shivered. The water was actually quite cold.

'We're moving,' observed Andrew. 'Can't you feel the current? Do you think it's to do with the island sinking? I hope we're not going to be dragged down with it.'

'No, it's pulling the other way,' said Sarah.

'It's getting very strong,' said Peter.

'Do you reckon the volcano's started a tsunami, or something?' Andrew wondered.

Whatever the reason, such was the strength of the current that soon all three were feeling less as though they were in the sea and more that they were in a fast-flowing river. Distant clouds began noticeably to turn. Faster and faster the clouds went, until they were no more than streaking blurs in the sky. The sunlight became a kaleido-scope of dizzy colours. There was a rushing noise in the children's ears and the whole universe seemed to be racing by at immense speed. All consciousness of the water was swallowed up in an endless flashing stream of light.

Then, suddenly, abruptly, they heard a voice.

'Hoi, there! What are you kids doing in that land drain?'

'Wha . . . What? Who are you?' gasped Peter.

'Who am I? I'm the lighthouse inspector. That's who.

And you've no right to be messing around with land drains. Now get out of it, all of you.'

Peter gazed up at the man. He found himself sitting in a brick-lined hole in a puddle of cold water. It wasn't very comfortable at all. Next to him, looking equally damp, were Sarah and Andrew.

With an effort he pulled himself out of the hole, feeling more than a little sheepish. His brother and sister did the same, all muttering, 'Sorry,' to the irate lighthouse inspector.

'All right,' he smiled. 'Well, it looks like you've got yourselves thoroughly soaked. Teach you a lesson, mucking about in drains. Never know what you might catch. Go on, be off with you. Go and have your adventures somewhere else.'

'We're back,' said Sarah, as they walked down the hill on to the path. 'But I wish we weren't.'

'I wonder how long it'll be?' mused Andrew.

'I want to understand that book,' said Peter.

Just then they heard a cry overhead. A bright yellow-hammer chirped out its morning call: '*A-little-bit-of-bread-and-no-cheese.*' Or was it, '*You'd-better-come-quick. You'd-better-come-quick. You'd-better-come-quick – pleeese?*'

Sarah looked down at her soaking wet trainers and laughed. 'I knew they'd get messed up if we followed Andrew,' she said.

Oswain and the Battle for Alamore
(Book One)

Discover the secret of Oswain's past
and the awesome power of the
Merestone.

Join Peter, Andrew and Sarah, with
Prince Oswain and Trotter the
badger, as they struggle against the
evil tyrant Hagbane in this fast-
moving, action-packed story of the
battle between good and evil.

'. . . as exciting and tense as Harry Potter' – Shaun Milward, aged 10

Oswain and the Mystery of the Star Stone
(Book Two)

Powerful forces are on the move . . .
Princess Alena has run away, wearing
the precious Star Stone. Gublak the
goblin wants the Star Stone more than
anything else in the world.
Meanwhile, Peter, Sarah and Andrew
are having trouble with pirates.

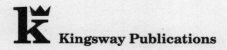 **Kingsway Publications**

Oswain and the Quest for the Ice Maiden

(Book Three)

Big trouble is brewing in Kraan as Surin's army prepares for war. The chief sorcerer of the order of Thorn has offered the king his long-awaited chance to take vengeance on the South. If he succeeds Oswain and his kingdom will be destroyed. Oswain's only hope is to find the Ice Maiden before it is too late.

Peter and Sarah join him in a dramatic race against time. Meanwhile Andrew and his scruffy dog Tatters seek help from Karador and his band of fugitive slaves.

The fate of the free world hangs in the balance as the tiny company stands against the combined might of Surin's army and the sorcerer's schemes.

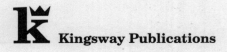
Kingsway Publications